Deadly Sin

ANGUS BRODIE AND MIKAELA FORSYTHE MURDER MYSTERY
BOOK SIXTEEN

CARLA SIMPSON

#204 ON THE STRAND, LONDON

I STEPPED DOWN from the coach, Aunt Antonia's driver having delivered me back to the office after our latest afternoon adventure viewing a potential residence after the loss of the townhouse to fire some months earlier.

I say *adventure*, as these forays about London had begun to resemble some of my more interesting adventures during my travels.

There was Covington House some weeks earlier, a monument to the late Lord Arthur Covington, with his penchant for collecting Middle Eastern artifacts from his own travels before his untimely death at the age of ninety-four.

There had been a very interesting sword that had once belonged to Genghis Khan, according to the estate manager. Lily, who shared my appreciation for swords, would have loved it.

However, she was presently in Edinburgh after receiving a rather ominous letter from an old acquaintance of her former life before I brought her to London after a previous inquiry case.

While I had not approved of her taking herself off, Brodie had reminded me that she was of an age where she could make decisions for herself. And she was now in the company of his friend Munro, who had appointed himself guardian.

That was some consolation, as she could be quite impetuous and headstrong, and while she might be of an age at almost twenty years, a young woman on her own...

Brodie had also reminded me that I had also taken myself off on my travel adventures at an early age. The shoe very much now on the other foot.

I had also visited the former residence of Sir William McMannis, a once highly regarded merchant with international trade connections.

There was a bit of a scandal several years before when it was rumored his company encountered some financial difficulties discovered by his associate, who disappeared and was eventually found buried in the gardens of McMannis Manor.

Sir William was arrested when evidence was discovered about his involvement, eventually sent to trial, and was presently serving time in prison.

Brodie had accompanied me on that inspection of McMannis Manor and commented afterward regarding other bodies that might be buried there. I had declined further interest in the residence.

He refused to accompany me further in our search for a residence after pointing out that he could live anywhere. Case in point, the small flat that adjoined the office on the Strand.

There also remained my great aunt's invitation that we might take up residence with her at Sussex Square. I suspected Brodie would not be in favor of that.

He was fond of Aunt Antonia. They had quite a lot in common. There was a smuggler or two in the family, along with a highwayman who was quite notorious. Brodie had his own past exploits surviving on the streets of Edinburgh before arriving in London with Munro. Still...

I thanked her as her driver, Mr. Hastings, guided the coach onto the street. I was rapidly coming to the conclusion that we might be making the office our permanent residence.

Mr. Cavendish, who had become a trusted associate, wheeled out from the adjacent tobacco shop on his platform, Rupert the hound trotting along behind. The owner of the shop often had a cookie or biscuit for the hound, a reward for guarding the shop at night, as well as the office.

"Afternoon, Miss," Mr. Cavendish greeted me.

"Mr. Brodie has not returned?" I inquired as I knelt on the sidewalk and scratched the hound's ears.

Brodie had departed quite early, informing me that he had an appointment after learning that Aunt Antonia had another residence we might want to see today. At the time, I had my suspicions about that sudden 'appointment.'

"Not as yet. That appointment did seem important. He said it would take some time."

"Yes, of course."

"There was a lad, one of those newspaper runners, wot brought round a message for you earlier. I put it in the letterbox for you, up at the office."

I thanked him and entered the lift, Rupert at my side. He was an excellent protection dog; however, I was not fooled that he was protecting me now from some unseen menace.

The hound was an excellent forager and no doubt was hoping for one of the biscuits left from breakfast earlier. Upon reaching the second-floor landing, I retrieved the envelope from the letterbox.

The envelope was plain, with my name in a hasty scrawl

that was familiar. It appeared to have been sent by Theodolphus Burke, reporter for the Times newspaper.

He had acquired a reputation for the daily articles that appeared in the scandal sheet that had exposed some of the most sensational gossip and criminal activities across the city.

We had crossed paths in the past when I had inquired about information from the newspaper archives and previous articles he had written, while making inquiries for a client. He had taken to attempting to pry information from me as well. Not that I trusted him.

He was unscrupulous and untrustworthy for the most part, interested only in furthering his status and career, along with the ambition of one day writing his own novel about his time in the newspaper business.

He was not particularly liked by those in Parliament or the Royal family, with articles that exposed secrets and scandals.

The Prince of Wales had once described him as 'a pox upon decent people' after a particularly scathing article about the Prince's 'private activities,' that had included my good friend Templeton.

"Marvelous," she had declared at the time. "That article will undoubtedly bring more patrons to the theatre."

As for my own experience with the man, he had been scathingly condescending of my Emma Fortescue novels, which he described as 'drivel for frustrated women,' as well as my inquiries in the cases Brodie and I pursued. I had particular thoughts about the man.

Brodie had reminded me, somewhat amused, that such action was referred to as '*murder*,' and would no doubt see me thrown into prison. I had informed him that I might very well be awarded a medal by the Prince of Wales for it.

And here I was now, staring suspiciously at an envelope

that he had obviously sent, as I sat at my desk with the hound sprawled at my feet as he devoured the remnants of that earlier breakfast that Mr. Cavendish had brought over from the Public House.

I was tempted to simply toss the letter into the rubbish bin beside Brodie's desk after other notes Burke had sent in the past:

"How are your inquiries progressing regarding Lady Ainsworth and her affair with that young military officer her daughter is betrothed to?"

And another:

"What of the missing bank funds after the disappearance of the bank president? New material for your next novel?"

What new insult was contained in Burke's latest note?

I stared at the envelope for the longest time. I should throw it away as I had the others—however, there was that saying about curiosity and the cat.

I seized the envelope, opened it, and pulled out the note.

"I have a proposition for you, Emma Fortescue. Meet me at the Old Bell this evening. And do not be late."

There was also a time noted. Arrogant, miserable... As if his time were so very valuable. I stared at the note.

Most curiously, he had used my pen name for my novels. Was it merely nothing more than one of his insults in his search for information for an article he was writing regarding a recent inquiry case?

I paced the office. That note was much like a banner being

waved before a bull in the arena I had seen on my travels through Spain. I vividly remembered how that had ended, thoroughly disgusted by the 'sporting event,' as it was called.

I glanced at it once more. A ruse, no doubt, to further his own ambitions. Still, the way he had worded it...

The Old Bell tavern was on Fleet Street, very near the Times offices. It was a favorite of Burke's, where he could be seen indulging in the adulation of those of his profession. Over pints of ale, amid stories he told of his own adventures reporting the daily news.

It was very near the time Burke had said to meet him at the Old Bell.

I gathered my travel bag, tucked the note into it, and locked the office door behind me. On the street below, I had Mr. Cavendish wave down a cab.

"What shall I tell Mr. Brodie?" he inquired.

What indeed? After previous incidents, he would no doubt find it interesting that I had gone to meet Burke. And equally, would not approve, particularly because I had done so alone, and at that time in the evening.

"A quick errand," I replied. No doubt I would return shortly, very likely before Brodie.

The hound waited expectantly as the driver arrived, and I opened the door of the coach.

"Not this time," I told him with a hand to prevent him jumping inside.

Although it was quite tempting to take him along. He had a particular dislike for Burke. However, I was most curious what the *'proposition'* he had mentioned in the note might be, and the hound rarely hesitated when he disliked someone.

Rupert sat on the sidewalk with what could only be interpreted as a grumpy expression at being left behind as I gave the driver the destination of the Old Bell on Fleet Street.

It was not far, however the street in front of the tavern was quite congested.

"There seems to be a bit of commotion, miss," my driver commented as he pulled to a stop down the street. "I might say, not a place for a lady this time o' the night."

Commotion indeed, as a crowd had gathered on the sidewalk, what appeared to be customers of the Old Bell spilling out of the tavern, more than one man with a tankard in hand. Along with those who had gathered from the street, as shouts came amid the commotion. I stepped down from the coach and overheard several comments as I approached.

"Never saw the like..."

"He must have insulted the wrong person...again."

Where was Burke? Had he already arrived? Was he somewhere inside the tavern, or among those who had pushed their way onto the street?

I was jostled about as I elbowed through those who had gathered to the center of the crowd, amid other comments and the smell of stale ale and cigarette smoke. As I reached a slight parting of those gathered there, I glimpsed someone slumped on the sidewalk and stared down at the bloodied body.

It was Burke!

Was it a brawl? Some insult that someone else had taken offense to?

"What happened?" a man nearby asked.

"It's about time to my way of thinkin'..." Someone else replied. "Less competition for the rest of us."

"Someone cut him! Anyone see who it was?"

Not a brawl. Burke had been attacked, and the blood I saw was from a knife wound!

He was alive, that sneering gaze meeting mine through the chaos of bystanders and gawkers.

"Emma Fortescue," he whispered, a guttural sound as blood appeared on his lips. He gestured for me to come closer, a surprisingly strong grip closing around my wrist as he thrust a stained note into my hand.

"Take it!" he snarled. "You're the only one who can see it done!"

He coughed, a wretched sound filled with blood, as his head fell back to the sidewalk with a dying challenge.

"What...will you do now, Emma Fortescue?"

The shrill sound of the police whistle cut through the cold night air and the taunts and cruel jokes as he stared blankly back at me.

Theodolphus Burke, notorious reporter for the Times of London, was dead!

One

"THERE WAS A REVOLVER IN YOUR POSSESSION," the constable who sat across from me at the New Scotland Yard headquarters pointed out.

"And you were seen bending over the man, according to witnesses, Miss Forsythe."

"After he had already been wounded," I pointed out for the third time.

"What was your relationship with the victim?"

That particular question was far too tempting. My relationship with Burke?

Someone who had provided information on a past case, admittedly upon threat of dropping Burke to the floor. I had refrained from the temptation at the time.

"He provided information from time to time for inquiry cases I participate in with my associate."

"You were seen speaking with him."

Correction. "He spoke to me."

"What did he say?"

I thought that might be a little difficult to explain.

I replied instead, "He had asked me to meet him there."

"Did he say what it was about?"

A proposition? How was I to explain that?

"Do you have any idea what the motive for the attack might have been?"

No more so than the countless people across London that he managed to offend with his articles that exposed affairs, scandals, and all manner of bad deeds. However, I did not say that and instead replied that I did not.

"What can you tell me about the weapon you were found carrying?"

The revolver Brodie insisted I always carry when out and about, due to his experience on the streets.

"The man was obviously stabbed to death, not shot," I pointed out. "The revolver has not been fired."

I had been transported to the Yard in a police van, with several others who were 'detained,' an unforgettable experience, and then questioned about the incident at the Old Bell.

Upon arrival I had immediately requested to speak with Inspector Dooley, who had worked with Brodie when he was with the MET and on several of our inquiry cases.

He appeared now, a frown on his face.

"Lady Forsythe... I was only just informed that you were here." He turned to the constable who had been plying me with such insightful questions.

"What is the meaning of this, Constable Jeffers?"

He was handed the report that had been written up after my arrival.

"Are there others in custody?"

"A half-dozen others were brought to the Yard who claimed to have seen the episode, sir. And several others who were present at the tavern afterward."

"Then I suggest you see to them."

"But, sir..."

"Lady Forsythe and her associate, Mr. Brodie, are consultants to the MET. I suggest that your attention be best directed to the others who were brought in."

Constable Jeffers quickly rose from behind the desk, nodded to Mr. Dooley and left.

Mr. Dooley had made inspector two years previous, and in return, we had provided him with information on other cases that came to the MET.

He was Irish, with sandy red brows over a blue gaze, thinning hair, and a bristly red moustache that twitched when he was excited.

"Knee-deep in murder once more, is it, Lady Forsythe?"

"So it would seem."

He nodded. "Contacted Brodie as soon as I was made aware that you were here. You do have a habit of popping up in the most difficult situations."

He had ordered coffee from another constable and explained that I was not a suspect and was to be given every courtesy, red moustache twitching when he then dismissed him.

"That will be all."

No sooner had he made that comment than Brodie arrived.

There is much to be said for knowing someone well—one's habits, reactions, which had often included disbelief, frustration, and obvious questions with a healthy dose of disapproval thrown in for good measure.

At that moment, I would have wagered on disbelief with a frown thrown in for good measure.

"I assume this has nothing to do with the manor ye were to visit today with her ladyship," he commented.

I assured him it did not, as Inspector Dooley arranged for me to leave, with a faint smile he attempted to hide beneath his moustache.

"It's not every man who must retrieve his wife from Scotland Yard," Brodie commented somewhat drily as we crossed the city after leaving the Yard.

"What the devil were ye thinkin', meetin' the man at the Old Bell?"

There were moments when all those years with the MET slipped into our conversations as I explained the note that I had received earlier from Burke requesting for us to meet, and then that blood-stained note with the name of a woman in St. John's Wood.

At present, I was beginning to feel as though I was being interrogated once again, after I had already provided the details to the constable and then to Mr. Dooley.

"Obviously not a social call, considerin' the man's reputation," Brodie replied. "Wot about when ye arrived?"

I explained the scene in front of the Old Bell with Burke already seriously injured, and that irritating challenge even as he lay dying.

"Do ye have any thought what he meant?"

"What will you do now, Emma Fortescue?"

"It seemed very odd," I admitted. "Very much like a challenge."

"Who the devil is Adele DeMille at St. John's Wood?" Brodie demanded.

I was aware of the name. "An actress at the Drury, as I recall, in a play last year—*As You Like It*."

He looked at me as if I might have taken a step away from sanity.

"The name of the play," I explained. "Though I do not recall any recent roles." Although I did not keep up with those things, aside from my acquaintance with my friend Templeton.

"It was obviously important enough that Burke wanted me to have the information, and it may have something to do with his murder."

"Then ye are determined to learn more in spite of the fact that the man had a good many enemies, any one of whom might have wanted him dead."

We were still 'discussing' the merits of making our own inquiries when we arrived at the office.

"There was a reason he wanted me to have that information," I pointed out, disgusting and unscrupulous as the man was.

"It could be helpful to the investigation by the MET," I added to make my point. "We will most certainly make Mr. Dooley aware of anything we learn.

"It would seem reasonable to visit St. John's Wood and see what we might learn from Adele DeMille. Or we might simply continue our search for an appropriate residence. Aunt Antonia did mention that she knew of still another residence in St. James's, which might be available."

We had reached the office. Brodie's response was a muttered curse, his opinion of that notion as he poured us both a dram of my Aunt Antonia's very fine whisky.

"We'll go to St. John's Wood in the morning."

I smiled to myself. There was usually more than one way around a grumpy Scot.

~

It was late morning when we arrived at St. John's Wood, a rural village that was home to artists, writers, and those seeking privacy, with tree-lined streets among green fields. Far different from the city proper, with crowded streets, soot-filled air, and ever-present fog from the river.

It was also removed from central London, where men of means and title kept their mistresses, including, according to rumor written by Theodolphus Burke in a previous scandal sheet article, the current mistress of His Royal Highness.

The postal office, across from quaint shops, a small art gallery, and a coffeehouse with tables set about the flagstone courtyard, seemed the place to begin our search for information about Adele DeMille. However, the clerk did not recognize the name. Obviously not a patron of the London theatre.

"The grocer might know. There would be deliveries," Brodie suggested. He had Mr. Jarvis, our driver, take us to a shop across the main square from the coffeehouse.

A woman who reminded me of Miss Effie at the Public House across from the office on the Strand greeted us as we entered.

"I know the name," she replied. "My Robbie delivers regular to Hampton Place, The next street over and out near the park. The bill is always paid on time, though I doubt she pays it herself.

"Calls herself an actress. Keeps to herself, that one. Usually sends round a list of what she wants for the day, though we've not received it this mornin'." She leaned in close and gave me a secretive look.

"She has visitors, if you know what I mean, and has ordered up some French wine that we had a devil of a time finding, expensive as well. I've seen her from time to time out and about. She visits the gallery across the way, and she's been seen at the coffeehouse as well.

I inquired how long she had lived at Hampton Place.

"Must be goin' on a full year now, lives mighty well for an actress, if you ask me."

"How would ye describe her?" Brodie inquired.

"She's not as tall as you," she directed the comment at me. "Slender, but well-proportioned in the right places, if you get my meanin'. Blonde hair, pretty enough, though I wouldn't bet that it's her own color, brown eyes, real private-like.

"What reason might ye be looking for her?" she asked again, curious, and no doubt eager for the latest gossip.

Instead of a direct reply, Brodie thanked her for the information.

We now had the location where Adele DeMille lived, and apparently 'entertained.'

Brodie gave Mr. Jarvis the woman's description of where Adele DeMille lived when we returned to the coach.

Absent the usual congestion of London streets, it was only a short ride to Hampton Place, a discreet distance from the village, according to directions Mr. Jarvis obtained from an attendant at the street cafe where a handful of men gathered for late morning coffee.

The manor at Hampton Place was set back from the street discreetly behind a stand of trees and a stone wall fence with wrought-iron gate.

Brodie had Mr. Jarvis wait across the street as we left the coach and approached that gated entrance.

The manor was red brick with white stone in the Georgian style, with tall windows that looked out on well-kept gardens. A flagstone circular drive for guests boasted statues of two life-sized lions, one at each side of the steps that led to those double doors.

No one arrived as we announced ourselves with the bell pull, nor were there any lights within to be glimpsed through the glass-paned door panels.

"Out about the village?" I suggested the possibility.

"Perhaps," Brodie replied, and then tried the latch at one of the doors.

"Or perhaps not," he added as the door slowly swung open.

Brodie announced our arrival as we stepped to the entrance of the manor. Once again, there was no response.

A long hallway led from the entrance, with rooms on each side. Double doors to the left opened onto an elaborate dining room with a table and a dozen chairs for guests.

A carved door to the right of the hall stood slightly ajar. Brodie reached back stopping me as he opened the door to a large parlor. The room had been completely turned over.

A chair before the hearth sat on its side, the satin brocade seat cut, layers of horsehair padding gaping through the opening. A side table had been toppled to the floor, and a mahogany cabinet stood with glass doors ajar, the contents strewn across the carpet.

"Someone was looking for something," I commented.

"So it would seem," Brodie replied.

Whoever had been there, the search was not confined to the parlor. The small adjacent library had fared no better.

Books had been pulled from the shelves and lay scattered open on the floor. The drawers of a desk were turned out. Upholstered chairs with padded arms and seats had been cut open as we discovered in the parlor.

We both turned at a startled sound from a young woman

who now stood in the doorway with a stunned expression. By the clothes she wore, she was obviously a maid.

"Are you with the police?" she asked. "I heard they were here."

"We work with the police," Brodie replied. "Who might ye be?"

"Bridget Dunham. I'm Miss Adele's maid," she replied.

She stood just inside the entrance still uncertain as she stared about the parlor.

"She's gonna be right upset when she sees this," she commented.

She seemed to lose some of her first wariness at finding us there.

She explained that she had been employed the past year by Adele DeMille. Who, it seemed, had disappeared.

"Did ye see or hear the intruders?" Brodie then asked.

She shook her head. "I haven't been here. Me mum hasn't been well and I needed to see to her. Miss Adele told me to take the days off and come back when she was better."

Brodie turned a chair right side up for her.

"When did ye last see Miss DeMille?"

"It was four, no five, days ago," she replied, looking at the chaos in the parlor with wide eyes.

"She had me help her get ready for guests she was expectin' that night. That's when she told me to take care of me mum. Has somethin' happened to her?"

Brodie and I exchanged a look.

"Did she say who those guests were?" he asked. "A name perhaps?"

She shook her head. "She never talked about the men that came here, said it was not for me to know."

"What can you tell us about her?" I inquired.

"She's an actress, I heard, performed on the stage in London before she came here. Said it was better than living on a few coins she was paid. And then there were the men that came here." Her cheeks colored.

"She liked the finer things. While I fixed her hair and helped her dress before they arrived, she would talk about plays she'd been in, the Paris theatre, and that she was never going back to that."

I kept mental notes and asked more questions while Brodie searched the rest of the residence.

Had Miss DeMille spoken of being afraid of anyone? Had there been any other situations like this before?

"No, miss," she replied.

What about other servants? A cook or housekeeper?

"She had a woman come in regular to clean, and Mrs. Haggerty prepared food when she was expecting friends. Jimmy in the village sees to it that she has a coach when she wants to go out."

Adele DeMille had obviously disappeared, quite unlike her. "Was it possible that she had gone to London?"

"Oh, no, miss," the girl replied. "She didn't care for London proper, said more than once that everything she needed was right here." She shook her head as she looked about.

"She's goin' to be upset about this. I hope there's nothing gone wrong. She said she could help me get a part in a play. I'd like that. I don't want to be a maid the rest of my life. I'd like to travel, work on the stage could provide that.

"I'll need to let Mrs. Nesby know about this. Such a shame. And the lock will have to be fixed." She shook her head as she left.

"What about the upstairs rooms?" I asked Brodie after she had gone.

"It could be useful to search them. There might something that might tell us what happened here."

There were four bedchambers on the second floor. Brodie took the rooms at the far end of the hall, while I took the two rooms nearest.

The first room I entered was sparsely furnished, with only a bed, and did not appear to have been disturbed.

The second bedchamber was much larger and had been turned over much the same as the library and parlor.

Bed linens had been stripped from the bed, drawers searched, as well as the armoire that once contained ladies' gowns and shoes, the entire contents now scattered across the floor.

On the dressing table were things a woman would keep—a lady's hairbrush, a jar of cream, and other cosmetics, as well as a crystal perfume bottle with a label from Paris. The fragrance was subtle: lavender and rosemary with a hint of citrus and vanilla.

My friend Templeton was known to indulge in fragrances from France, this one among them.

"There are scents for...shall we say, encouraging one's companion," she had explained, that made me think of that somewhat explicit painting on the headboard of her bed at her country residence.

I also discovered a package of *'French letters,'* protection for intimacy between a man and woman. From what the maid told us, as well as what I had discovered, it did seem that Adele entertained 'guests' in that manner. That would perhaps explain not only the discreet location but the richly furnished manor and obviously, guests of some financial means. With at least one who paid for where she lived as well as those gowns and fine perfume?

As I turned to leave, something gleamed from the carpet at the edge of the bed in the light that spilled into the room through the windows of the bedchamber. A piece of jewelry lost amid the search for something in the room. It appeared to be gold.

I picked it up. It was a gold button with what appeared to be the embossed figure of an animal. Not the sort of button a woman would have on a gown, but the sort that a man might have on a waistcoat or long coat.

Not unusual, I supposed, as it was obvious Adele DeMille 'entertained' gentlemen companions.

Yet it could be important. Did it belong to an acquaintance whom she had entertained? Or had it been lost as the room was turned over?

I searched for anything else that might tell us something about what had happened in that room, but found nothing more. Only that gold button and the obvious items of an intimate nature.

"Did ye find anything?" Brodie asked from the doorway to the chamber.

"It appears that she lived quite lavishly, and there was at least one gentleman who made regular visits." I held the package of 'French letters' aloft.

"Yer assuming it was a gentleman?" Brodie replied.

"So it seems. I also found this." I showed him the gold button.

He inspected the button.

"It's not the sort of decoration for a woman's garment, but more for a gentleman's waistcoat."

"Aye. And most certainly not what a police inspector,

merchant, or writer like those we saw earlier, might be able to afford."

"Did you find anything that might be useful?" I inquired.

"The other rooms have been thoroughly turned over as well," he replied. "It would seem that whatever the person was searching for, they failed to find."

We returned downstairs.

"And it would seem that either the woman was aware there might be some difficulty or returned afterward and left. There is no indication of an assault."

The question now was, what had changed regarding her obviously well-kept arrangement?

How was her disappearance and what we had found at that residence in St. John's Wood connected to Burke? Where had Adele DeMille disappeared to? For what reason? What was she afraid of?

Two

THE REMNANTS LEFT from a takeaway supper from the Public House had long been consumed by Rupert after we returned from St. John's Wood.

At present, he lay before the coal stove, snoring as he dozed, while I stood before the chalkboard after making my notes. A late edition of the Times newspaper lay open at Brodie's desk.

He had purchased a copy from one of the newsboys on the street after we returned. There was no mention of Burke's murder on the crime page or anywhere else in the newspaper, which seemed to indicate that word of his death had not reached the Times offices.

Mr. Dooley had spoken of keeping the attack from the newspapers as long as possible, with the hope that his attacker might assume that he had not succumbed to his wounds and possibly draw the murderer out. Brodie thought it highly unlikely.

"It could be useful...however, as time passes word will eventually leak, particularly with Burke's reputation and among others in the newspaper business," he pointed out. "The man was always looking for the next story, and this one will be most sensational."

He was right of course. As much as I disliked Burke, he had quite the reputation for gossip and the kind of scandal that people seemed addicted to, not unlike a narcotic.

"It could be helpful to visit his office at the Times," I suggested. "There might be a clue there that would tell us something. I'll go early in the morning when there are fewer staff about before the other reporters arrive for the day."

"And then there is this," Brodie held up the gold button with that unusual, embossed design that I had found in Adele DeMille's bedchamber.

"Might ye have seen it before? Does it mean anythin' to ye?"

I admitted that it did not.

"It's not unusual to find them on a gentleman's waistcoat. The Prince of Wales has a penchant for them with the initials HRH embossed on them. I suppose in the event someone needed to be reminded who he is."

"That information no doubt from yer friend, Templeton?" Brodie commented.

"She was quite amused by it. It seems that all of the buttons on his great coat and waistcoat were gold and embossed with those same letters. I did wonder if his under-drawers might also have gold buttons."

"Ye have an interest in His Highness's drawers?" he inquired with that smile at one corner of his mouth.

"I suspect it might be quite an ordeal to be rid of them when necessary," I replied, ignoring the obvious smirk.

"Although I suppose they could be quite valuable to a collector of such things—such as Fabergé eggs, a bauble Marie Antoinette might have worn, or some other rare gemstone."

"Ye are a wicked woman, Mikaela Forsythe."

I smiled to myself. "I do try."

"There are no initials on this button that might tell us something," he commented, inspecting it under the light from the electric lamp on his desk. "But it does have what looks verra like the image of an animal, possibly a dog."

I had noticed that as well when I found it. It had reminded me of something, although I couldn't quite remember what or where I might have seen something like it.

"Perhaps the man who owns the coat considers himself a hunter, like those ye know who chase around after a poor fox," he speculated.

Perhaps.

There was someone who might recognize it. My great aunt.

I would call on her and see if she had seen that embossed image before.

"What of Inspector Dooley?" I asked. "You did promise to let him know if we learned anything. "

"He'll be gone by now at end of day," Brodie replied. "I'll pay him a visit in the morning. He may have something that could be useful with our inquiries as well. And there could be something to be learned from the patrons at the Old Bell at night."

"The police did question them," I pointed out.

"Aye, but they might remember something more with one of their own, there for a pint or two."

Such as a man who was very accomplished at blending in, sharing a drink, picking up gossip on the street or in a tavern?

There were occasions when Brodie and I worked separately on an inquiry. As I knew well enough, two could be far more efficient than merely one person following leads and clues.

I rose early; however, Brodie was already gone, with the intention of meeting with Inspector Dooley before he began work for the day. As for myself, I was determined to visit Burke's office at the Times early as well, when there would be fewer about who might question my presence.

I dressed, collected my bag with pen and notebook inside, then set the lock to the office. The hound greeted me on the sidewalk with a lick of the hand, no doubt in search of a biscuit—cheeky fellow.

"Morning, miss," Mr. Cavendish greeted me. "Mr. Brodie said you were to have this." He handed me the morning edition of The Times newspaper.

"Will you be needing a driver?"

I nodded as I opened the paper and immediately turned to the crime sheet and quickly scanned it. There was nothing about the attack on Burke. I then turned to the scandal page and discovered the same.

There were no glaring headlines about Burke's death, no top sheet announcement of the grisly murder that had robbed the city of a valuable source of information, even when that information was often glaringly lacking in factual information. Such was Burke's reputation.

Mr. Cavendish had waved down a driver, Mr. Jarvis, who accompanied me on a good many of my travels across London. I gave him the destination of the Times offices on Fleet Street, then climbed inside.

When we arrived, I directed him to an adjacent street where we would be less conspicuous and asked him to wait.

I stepped down and waited in the alcove of a shop that was

not yet open and watched the entrance of the Times for several moments.

As I was about to step off the sidewalk, a coach pulled up to the entrance and a man stepped down. I immediately recognized Arthur Walter, the publisher of The Times, whom I had met previously.

I waited until he had entered the building. Inside the foyer, he exchanged a brief conversation with the young attendant.

I waited until Mr. Walter had entered the hallway toward the lifts that would take him to the second floor. As he disappeared, I crossed the street and entered the building.

The attendant looked up and smiled a greeting.

"Good morning, miss. You're out bright and early."

I smiled as well with the excuse I had planned for just such an encounter. "An advertisement that I want to place."

"Ah, yes, that would be at the third floor. Mr. Henry can assist you.

Then, on the chance that it might provide information, "Is Mr. Burke about this morning?"

That grin once more. "Not as yet. He was working a story that's kept him out and about of late."

"Yes, of course."

That told me two things—if Mr. Walter knew what had happened to his most popular reporter, the king of the scandal sheets, there was no indication that this young man was aware.

Admittedly, it was only a matter of time, of course. The longer Burke was absent, the more likely the truth would be discovered.

It also told me that Burke had been spending considerable time chasing down a story. Was that story the one about Adele DeMille that he had been so keen for me to know about?

I thanked the young man and turned toward the stairs instead of the lift.

The stairwell connected to the landing on the second floor very near Burke's private office. It was also some distance apart from the publisher's office.

I paused before reaching the second floor and listened for any sounds that might come from the floor and the reporters' gallery just beyond. It was quiet, and I continued the last few steps up to the landing.

I had previously been to Burke's office when I had attempted to learn information about a particularly difficult case. Burke had been his usual impossible self, with one deprecating remark after another, along with his usual scathing comment about a 'woman's place.'

That had not gone over particularly well. Still, as I now approached the door to his office, there was a sense of great loss.

Depending on how one looked at it, it could be said that Burke had either elevated the art of journalism, or possibly not. In the very least, he caused people to read the newspaper, most particularly his comments about society in general and the scandals he exposed. And in spite of his condescending remarks toward me, he had once provided a rather backhanded compliment.

"I do look forward to our encounters, Lady Forsythe. You are the only woman I have ever encountered who is well-read and can intelligently hold her own in conversation. But I will not divulge my source in the matter. I do have a reputation to maintain. As a matter of fact, I may write a book about my adventures."

As I say, condescending and full of himself.

With a glance in both directions down the hallway, I tried the latch on the door to his office. Not surprisingly, it was locked, no doubt when he departed for the Old Bell that night before, when I was to meet him.

I glanced about once more to make certain no one else was about.

I had acquired some unusual but useful skills working inquiry cases with Brodie. One of those was the ability to pick a lock. I removed a pin from my hair.

There was an obvious skill to picking a lock as he had pointed out, that required a calm manner, a sensitive touch, patience, and a good ear to hear the mechanisms inside a lock as they clicked, giving way one by one.

There were different types of locks—early ones that could be difficult because of time and the debris that made its way inside, although a well-worn lock might also easily give way. Then there were more modern locks that were improved with a complicated set of mechanisms that were often difficult to manipulate. However, a lock on a door inside a building often proved to open quite easily.

It seemed that Brodie was a master in the art of picking locks.

I heard two distinct clicks as I carefully worked the pin inside the lock, and *voilà*! The lock opened.

With a look about to make certain that I hadn't been discovered, I pushed open the door and quickly stepped inside the office.

There was a shade on the inside window that looked out onto the hallway. I carefully pulled it down so as not to be seen, then turned to Burke's desk.

It was covered with scattered papers—a torn-off calendar

page from two days earlier, scribbled reminders to himself on a calendar on the desk pad, as well as notes he'd received, and others he'd made in a hasty scrawl.

At the risk of being caught, I turned on the desk lamp and started my search with the calendar pages, searching for any reference that might include that last evening at the Old Bell, as well as any reference to Adele DeMille.

More than once there was a sound beyond the door as someone passed by. I stopped, then began again.

Somewhat of a surprise, I discovered a receipt from Western Laundry Co., Fulham, among the scattered papers. It itemized several items of ladies' garments!

Did the receipt have something to do with Adela DeMille's disappearance?

To my knowledge, there was not a Mrs. Burke. And I couldn't imagine a female 'acquaintance' otherwise.

Although, as Brodie had previously pointed out about an acquaintance of his own, Mr. Brown, a known criminal sort, there might very well be a female companion tucked away somewhere.

What followed was a question as to whether I might be part of that distinguished sisterhood. Tucked away indeed!

With that half-smile that always meant there was more than what was being said, Brodie had informed me that one would hardly consider me to be 'tucked away.' He had then added that I was not the sort.

All well and good, yet I did wonder what 'sort' I was.

"Bothersome, headstrong," he'd commented. "Someone who can burn water and with the habit of taking herself off into places she shouldn't."

I had ignored the rest of it. There was no arguing with a stubborn Scot. It was an argument I could not win.

I continued my search of Burke's desk and discovered a note on the desk calendar for a meeting at O.B. with M.F. Obviously a reminder of his meeting with myself at the Old Bell. I then searched the desk drawers.

One was filled with folders that contained copies of past columns he'd written, another, unsurprisingly, with two freshly laundered shirts. It seemed as though Burke might have lived at the Times' office. That might explain his somewhat scruffy appearance.

Then, completely unexpected, in the bottom drawer...a book! While Burke was somewhat intelligent, I did not consider him the sort who would read a book of an evening before a warm fire.

I half expected some dry tome about battle campaigns or the history of London as I retrieved it. I stared at the title on the cover:

The Case of the Missing Children,
a novel by E. Fortescue

It was one of my novels, with Emma Fortescue as my main character! Written after I began participating in inquiry cases with Brodie!

To say that I was surprised was a vast understatement, particularly given Burke's opinion of my writing efforts and what he had described as 'woman's drivel.'

I hesitated, then opened it and discovered something that was an even greater shock. He had made notes in the margins on several pages. The comments varied from criticism to what might have been considered reluctant praise—*'somewhat entertaining.'*

I didn't take the time to read further—there was too much

risk of being discovered. I stuffed the novel into my travel bag along with the receipt and the desk calendar, with the hope that they might tell me more.

I then searched the cabinet behind the desk, yet found nothing there that might be helpful. I glanced at the wall clock. I had been there for more than half an hour, and by this time more staff would be arriving for their morning shift.

At another sound from the hall, I turned off the electric lamp and waited for any additional sound that someone lingered outside.

I heard nothing more and quickly gathered my travel bag, went to the door and listened again before stepping out into the hallway.

There was the faint sound of conversation from the reporters' floor, only a handful of steps beyond. I glanced toward the stairwell.

Anyone at the gallery could easily see me as I left. I hesitated, then turned the opposite direction that led away from Burke's office, past two other doors, and then to that single door at the end of the hallway.

More than once Burke had escaped meeting with me by the very same door that I knew opened out of the building to a set of iron stairs that led to the alleyway below. I had silently cursed him at the time.

However, I was now grateful for that escape as I stepped out onto the wrought-iron landing. I descended the steps to the alleyway below, where newsboys had gathered to collect the late morning edition of the newspaper to be sold on the streets.

I ignored their curious stares and continued around the corner to the street and returned to my waiting coach.

"Good to see you, miss," Mr. Jarvis greeted me. "Had a

constable pass by a while ago and tell me that I would need to move on when he came back round."

I climbed aboard and gave him the address of the laundry company in Fulham.

"Not a proper area for some," he commented. "And some distance this late in the morning."

Nevertheless, I insisted.

Along with Mr. Cavendish, it did seem that Brodie might have something to do with Mr. Jarvis's comment. Not a place for my sort!

With the usual street traffic found across all of London, it was well past midday when we finally arrived at Broughton Road. It teemed with the usual traffic of wagons and carts, along with vans with the company name painted on the side that arrived as others departed, no doubt for afternoon deliveries.

Mr. Jarvis maneuvered the coach through the congestion, cutting off another driver in the process with a colorful exchange of words as he refused to move the coach, and the other driver was forced to wait for traffic to open.

More comments followed, along with a V-gesture of the fingers, as the other driver finally moved past.

"Apologies, miss," he said as I stepped down from the coach. "There's some blokes that ain't got no manners. If you want me to come along...?"

With a smile to myself at the encounter, I assured him that it was not necessary.

"I'll be right here if there's a need."

The laundry was in a working-class area of London near the river, a large cut-stone building with signage at the entrance that indicated both laundry and dry- cleaning services for the

Grand Hotel and Brown's Hotel, as well as business professionals across London.

A woman appeared at the front counter.

"I'm hoping you can help me with some information."

I caught the look of surprise along with obvious curiosity. I showed her the receipt and asked if she could tell me where the laundry was to be delivered.

"We don't get many personal orders. Most come from the hotels and professional sorts. This was from a customer in the business district, Fleet Street."

She retrieved a ledger, found the receipt number, and looked up.

"Is there some problem with the order, miss?"

She appeared to assume the order had been for myself. I made up the excuse that I was concerned that it might have been lost.

"Can you tell me where it was to be delivered?"

"According to the customer's instructions the woman's clothes was to be delivered in Southwark, at Borough High Street. That would have been an extra run across the river, but the customer paid extra for it.

"The customer claimed the woman was not able to get out and about. The extra fee he paid more than covered the driver's time to have it delivered."

"Is the driver here now?"

"That be Tommy Noonan. He's not here now. Out on delivery to the hotels. They go through a lot of laundry with guests comin' in."

I wanted very much to speak with him. What might he be able to tell me about that delivery of women's clothes in Southwark?

"When will he return?"

"Not 'til the mornin', miss. He stays over in Holborn with a young woman, then picks up a wagonload full of dirty laundry early next day at the hotels."

"Do your records show when he made that delivery?"

"Two days ago, according to the delivery log. It woulda been before he made his first mornin' run. Is there something wrong with the order, miss?"

I thanked her for the information and returned to where Mr. Jarvis waited with the coach.

An address in Southwark. What did that mean?

It hardly seemed likely that Burke kept a flat there, when it appeared that he might very well live out of his office at the Times.

Was it merely a coincidence that the order included woman's garments?

Anyone else might assume the garments were for a lady friend. However, knowing Burke, I thought that highly unlikely.

He was the most aggravating, insulting, disgusting sort of man I had ever met. I could not imagine any woman who would put up with him. At one point, I had even questioned whether he had a mother.

As for a 'lady friend,' as the woman at the laundry suggested...

My imagination simply could not conjure that up.

Or did it have something to do with Burke's murder and what we had already discovered at St. John's Wood?

I inquired if Mr. Jarvis was familiar with Borough High Street in Southwark.

"I can find it, but it's a good distance across the river, and not a place for a lady to be out late in the day, if you get my meanin'," he replied. "And Mr. Brodie would not want you goin' there alone."

"You did say that you wanted to go to Sussex Square as well?" he reminded me. "There's enough time yet for that."

The day was rapidly fading as lights gleamed from the windows of the laundry, and there were long shadows on the street as daylight faded.

I was tempted to tell him to continue on. However, those shadows reminded me that I had told my great aunt earlier in a telephone conversation that I had questions in a new inquiry.

Those questions had to do with that gold button I had found at the residence in St. John's Wood.

"Very well," I replied and climbed into the coach.

It was early evening when I finally arrived at Sussex Square after stopping briefly at the office on the Strand.

According to Mr. Cavendish, Brodie had returned earlier, then left for the Old Bell, dressed in the clothes he wore when he intended to 'disappear,' as he called it.

There was no note in the office, nor had I expected one. I updated the chalkboard with what I had learned and then had Mr. Jarvis bring me to Sussex Square.

Mr. Symons, my great aunt's head butler, greeted me at the entrance.

"Her ladyship informed me that you would be arriving. Very good to see you again, Miss Mikaela."

"The formal parlor?" I inquired, her usual location late in the afternoon for what she called 'refreshment.' Refreshment, most usually meant a dram before supper was announced.

"She will join you there."

That could mean almost anything.

"Has she set off on one of her expeditions into the old fortress?"

Of late, she was determined to retrieve important artifacts from the part of her ancestors' fortress that adjoined the manor. She insisted that she was simply trying to put things in order among the artifacts.

"It is important to preserve old things. How else are you and Lenore, and Lily of course, and now Lenore's children, to know your ancestors and their importance in the scheme of things?" she had declared several months earlier.

"I am not getting any younger, you know, and there are some marvelous ancestors in the family. One day, someone will want to write about them."

This part of the conversation had been directed at myself. It was something she had suggested before. I had pointed out there was the official Montgomery record that was part of the royal archive.

"Of course, dear. However, that hasn't always included those who were born below the salt... Robbie FitzWarren, for example. The stories about him that I was told as a child! Quite a bounder! And not mentioned in the official family record at all. Brodie reminds me of him."

There had been other colorful characters that had been briefly mentioned in records, or not all.

"She has been occupied today with pictures. Out and about since the early hours. Mrs. Ryan has been quite exhausted with her roaming about. You know how she can be when she is occupied with something new, miss."

I did know, very well. However, that did not explain what the new project was, Mrs. Ryan's condition after following her about, or which pictures were in question.

Mr. Symons had been in service to my great aunt long before my sister and I arrived as children. He had never married and lived at Sussex Square.

He had considered us very near his own children to be watched over, and I owed him a great deal for his 'discretion' in the secrets he kept about my own early adventures. Such as when I had escaped through the window outside my room on the second floor rather than attend an extremely boring social event Aunt Antonia was hosting.

Linnie had been my co-conspirator in those adventures until she was caught in a very creative lie about where I was at the time.

More recently, Mr. Symons had become a reliable source. I could always rely on him to provide information about what my great aunt was up to, considering her advanced age and some of her own early adventures.

"She is quite spirited," he had observed on more than one occasion.

I thanked him now and continued on to the formal parlor, where tumblers and a decanter of Old Lodge awaited on a side table, along with a most interesting flat box the size of one of my books.

It was made of leather and wood with a small metal latch on the side. I pressed it and the box opened to reveal a lens mounted on a small extended leather bellows. It was a camera!

That explained Mr. Symons comment about 'pictures.'

There had been some remarkable developments in cameras, far different from the large, bulky ones on tripods that street photographers used or the ones used in photographers' studios.

"Here you are, dear!" Aunt Antonia announced as she swept into the parlor. "I needed to change into something more appropriate than my hunting costume for going out and about." She glanced at the side table.

"I see Mrs. Ryan has provided refreshment. I was quite concerned about her earlier. She was quite exhausted."

And then, "You've discovered my camera. A remarkable invention. It creates images on a roll of film that the fellow Kodak invented." She went to the side table and poured us both a dram of whisky.

She handed me a tumbler. "It's most entertaining. I cannot wait to see the photographs once they are..." she searched for the word.

"Developed?" I suggested.

"Yes, that is the word, some sort of chemical bath. I'm told any pharmacist attendant can provide that. Supposedly they have the appropriate materials." She paused.

"Do you suppose your friend, Mr. Brimley, might be able to accommodate? Charming man."

"Very possibly," I assured her, my thoughts already returning to my inquires of the day.

The camera was quite small. It would have been most convenient. I could have taken pictures of the items I discovered instead of taking them.

"You mentioned a new inquiry case in your telephone call this morning," she reminded me.

I retrieved the gold button we had found at St. John's Wood from the pocket of my walking skirt.

"What can you tell me about this?"

"Oh, dear. I shall need my reading glasses," she announced. "There at the hearth table. Odd. How is someone supposed to find their glasses when they need them to find something in the first place?"

Wisdom from someone who had finally admitted that she had some difficulty reading invitations to events, the dailies, and of course the scandal pages.

She had blamed it on bad handwriting from the sender of an invitation at the time, and then poor print at the newspaper, until Linnie convinced her that glasses were quite fashionable.

"I do not care whether they are the fashion or not," she had exclaimed.

Linnie had then pointed out that she might need them when driving her motor carriage about the streets of London.

"Quite true. The streets are often quite mucked up and signs difficult to read," Aunt Antonia had admitted. Which had raised another issue, about her adventures in the Benz motor carriage.

I had learned to pick the battles, and that was for another day. I found her glasses, wire-rimmed with a gold chain attached, and handed them to her.

"A button!" she exclaimed as she stared at it once her glasses were in place. "A man's coat button by the look of it, and most certainly made of gold. Most interesting." She looked up. "A clue in your inquiry, perhaps?"

Clever. Too clever at times, as she waited for more details, which I did not share at the moment.

"Of course, you cannot say at this time. I can tell you that it is well made, of the sort a gentleman might wear on his waistcoat, and...yes, just as I thought. It is undoubtedly real gold." She tossed back the hearty dram of whisky in her glass.

"Come along to the sword room, dear. There are some fascinating examples among your ancestors' costumes, including those of my father," she announced.

"He insisted on gold with the family crest," she explained as we rode the lift to the second floor.

"That is how you can tell authentic materials from those that are not, such as the ones that tailors use now for clients."

Those clients undoubtedly businessmen, professional customers of lesser means than a duke, or a king?

The sword room had always fascinated me, a collection of all things in a long history of our ancestors that included weapons—most particularly a fascinating collection of swords and a half dozen suits of armor, along with costumes decorated with medals, ribbons, and gold buttons.

"Gold buttons." She pointed to those on her father's red wool ceremonial coat, the same as in his portrait.

"This fell off when I had his clothes moved from the old part of the place." She picked up a button at a nearby table. "If you look on the reverse of the button you will find embossed letters..."

Three

BRODIE

HE MADE a telephone call to Inspector Dooley and met him at a coffeehouse away from the Yard.

They had shared what both had learned following Burke's murder outside the Old Bell.

"Our people questioned those we brought in. As to be expected, a good many of them didn't see the attack, only after it, when Burke was down. But there was something one person saw, a bystander in the crowd. A man who seemed particularly interested when Lady Forsythe arrived."

Brodie's attention sharpened.

"He said the man approached where she bent down beside Burke, in a manner that seemed curious at the time."

"How so?"

"Said it was almost as if the man knew her from the look on his face. The witness said it 'could have turned water to ice,' as he put it," Dooley replied.

"Knew her?" Brodie suggested.

Dooley nodded. "It's something to keep in mind."

"The man who saw him, what is his name?"

"Fitch. He works on road construction nearby where repairs are being made. He had stopped by the Old Bell end of day, as he usually does before going on home to the wife. Lives in a walk-up in Burley." He gave Brodie a meaningful look.

"Not that I shared this with you. Keep it to yerself."

He appreciated it. "What more was he able to tell ye about the man he saw?"

"Said he was built like someone who just stepped off of the boxing stage. No lightweight, experienced, and not the sort you would want to come up on in a dark alleyway."

"Or a tavern?"

Mr. Dooley nodded. "Burke's misfortune to cross the man's path. Most likely a typical robbery after a game of dice. A pity, although the man had a poor reputation about London, with the scandals and bribes he wrote about."

It was easy enough to *assume* that it might have been robbery. It happened often enough. But Burke was the sort who was wise to the ways of the street. His pursuit of that next story about a scandal could take him into the worst corners of London.

Burke boasted that he carried just enough coin to acquire information from his 'sources.' It was rumored that some of those sources came from inside the MET, a constable eager to make extra money in exchange for information. Dooley was aware of the rumors.

"Could it have been someone within?" Brodie saw the way Dooley's expression shifted. "If certain information became known in one of the man's articles?"

If caught, the constable or inspector was immediately released and could be brought up on charges. But it was a situation where passing information or the outside 'job' was lucrative enough to cover the possibility.

"Before you ask, there's no one at the Yard fits that description," Dooley had replied. "That doesn't account for others though, particularly any who might have been passed over for promotion or demoted in the outlying areas," Dooley added.

"I've got two of my people discreetly making inquiries."

Brodie nodded. If the man who had attacked Burke was from the 'inside,' he would eventually be found out, exposed, and the matter settled.

If the man were from the streets, it would be that much harder to find him. Unless he was the sort who needed to make certain the *job* that he'd been hired to do was, in fact, finished.

"The man disappeared quickly enough according to wot ye told me," Brodie commented.

Dooley nodded. "Like his tail was afire, according to the man, Fitch."

"And there's been no word put out by the MET or the newspapers yet about Burke's murder," he pointed out.

"If the man was scared off, there might be some doubt that Burke is dead. Where was the body taken?"

"I had it brought to the Yard under a John Doe. I thought it best until we have a lead on the murderer. I doubt that Burke is in any condition to protest. What about yourself?"

"I have inquiries I want to make on the street, then I'm for the Old Bell and perhaps a conversation with Mr. Fitch when he arrives."

"I'll send along a couple of the lads in their street clothes."

Brodie shook his head. "I thank ye just the same."

Dooley frowned. "I suppose there's no need to say it." Then he did.

"Be careful out there. You have a few that would like to

even the score from the old days. I'd not want to have to explain to Lady Forsythe that she's just been made a widow. She has a bit of a temper."

"Aye, that she does."

"Do ye still carry the revolver and that knife in yer boot?" Dooley asked.

After his meeting with Dooley, he slipped back out onto the street filled with the usual sounds and smells from the river with its refuse, garbage, and its secrets as he left the Yard. Along with the cold that had a way of burrowing under a man's coat, leaving that hollow feeling deep inside.

It was always there, waiting to pull him back...to places that he'd left behind not once, but twice.

Edinburgh, with a different cold that could freeze the flesh on a young lad who had gone hungry until he stole his next crust of bread or picked that next pocket.

Then afterward, London with a different kind of cold. The kind that reminded ye that ye were just another lost soul among others, with no importance except to yerself.

There had been another, like himself. They had watched each other's back, scraped, clawed, and bled for survival. Someone he trusted—Munro.

He was in Edinburgh, yet if he were there now, he would go to people he knew from the whisky trade he handled for Mikaela's great aunt for a name of someone who might know someone.

Brodie had his own sources. Faces with names they'd invented. He kept them at a distance with the work he did now —private inquiries—and for other reasons that had everything to do with *her*. Those who frequented the taverns and pubs, but had once walked the streets as he had.

He caught a ride on a tram with a route toward Holborn. Once there, he found a carter who provided a ride in the back of his cart for two pence. The address was familiar, along with the woman who swept the steps.

"Aye, he's about," she replied with a nod. "Most likely sleepin' it off. It was late when he returned last night. Ye'll need to pound extra hard on the door."

And then, taking her advice...

"Wot the devil! Are ye trying to raise the dead?"

When the door eventually opened, his friend from those days with the MET glowered at him from the doorway. Brodie stepped past him into the small flat that was what former Constable Jimmy Conner could afford on his police pension. Along with money he made on the side that provided ale in any one of a half dozen pubs across London, a place he knew well from thirty years in service, retired now for a handful more.

The cap of white hair and glaring blue gaze shot through with red matched the belligerent greeting. Jimmy Conner didn't wait for him to explain.

"The answer is *no*! I'm retired. I want nothing to do with the MET or...!" Conner jabbed a finger at his shoulder to make the point.

Brodie ignored the jab and the curses. "What about Theodolphus Burke?"

The rant stopped midway through a new round of curses.

"Burke?"

The history between the two men—Burke and his friend—was filled with accusations of police brutality and wrongdoing, then demotion with an article that named names on a crime sheet.

It was one of Burke's early campaigns to elevate his own importance by accusing the constable who made the arrest.

It cost his friend a promotion that he was up for at the time, and verra nearly his job.

As Brodie knew only too well, it was not a matter that was easily forgotten. He heard it again in the way Conner said the man's name.

"*Bratach salach*!" his friend spat out in Gaelic. "What is he up to now? Causing another good man to lose his reputation over lies just so he can promote himself?"

"He's dead."

That stopped Jimmy Conner midstream of more curses. His eyes narrowed with suspicion.

"Dead? The world could not be that fortunate!"

Brodie nodded.

"Dead?" Conner made a sound of approval. "It seems there is some justice in the world."

He motioned for Brodie to join him at a small table, where he offered him a drink.

"Coffee," Brodie replied. He wanted his friend sober.

"I won't say that it's a shame about Burke," Conner commented after several cups of coffee.

"To my way of thinkin', he had it comin'. But now there's a woman involved, ye say? It would seem there is more to this."

Brodie nodded. "Burke frequented the Old Bell. I'll be there this evening to learn what I can from a man who apparently saw the murderer.

"Inspector Dooley has Burke with a John Doe at the Yard, to keep everything quiet until we can learn wot this has to do with the woman that he seemed to think was important enough to give Mikaela that note."

He had told Conner the rest of it—what they had found

at that residence at St. John's Wood where the woman apparently 'entertained' a handful of men regularly, the condition of the manor when they arrived, and the woman's disappearance.

"And herself?" Conner inquired, no doubt meaning Mikaela, his expression softening. "In the middle of it as usual?"

Brodie nodded. "She was to go to Burke's office this morning to see if there was anything to be learned there."

"I can see you will be needing assistance, with Munro off to Edinburgh."

"Aye, from someone I can trust. With that note of Burke's, there's a connection to the woman. I need to find her. And I want the name of the man who killed Burke. By the description Inspector Dooley had, the man was the sort who works for someone else."

Conner nodded. "There might be something to be learned in one of the other fine establishments nearby."

Brodie nodded. "Mr. Dooley has put the word out about the attack, but made certain it's known that Burke survived."

Jimmy Conner nodded. "The man will want to know more and be askin' about."

The plan was set. "Watch yer back, lad."

Lad.

Brodie shook his head as he left Holborn and turned toward the Strand.

It had been that way from the beginning when he joined the foot patrol of the MET and first worked with Jimmy Conner, had supported him through the difficulty with Burke, and several years after.

No matter that he had made inspector and was Jimmy's superior. He still called him that—lad.

He finally reached the office with some time before he intended to go to the Old Bell. Mr. Cavendish nodded a greeting as he rolled up at the sidewalk, the hound with him.

"Miss Mikaela returned earlier and was up in the office for a time, then set off for Sussex Square."

Brodie nodded and took the stairs up to the second-floor landing. She had spoken about wanting to show that gold button to Lady Montgomery, who might recognize it.

He glanced at the chalkboard, then took a closer look. She'd added notes. One in particular stood out—the laundry receipt, and she'd managed to learn that it was delivered in Southwark?

End of day traffic in that part of London had thinned when he returned to the street and had Mr. Cavendish wave down a driver.

"The Old Bell, ye say guv'ner?" the driver replied. "A round or two to end the day?"

He nodded as he climbed into the cab.

"Right yer are," the driver added as they set off.

It was well into the evening when he signaled for the driver to stop short of pulling up before the pub and he stepped down. A 'worker,' dressed as he was, wouldn't pay for a driver when the coins could be spent on ale.

He pulled the billed cap low, walked the length of the street, then entered the pub.

It was the same as a hundred more across the city. The sounds, the smells, the smoke that filled the air from a pipe or cigarette. And the woman who cut through the tables with years of experience in the balance of a tray, a laugh at something that was said, and the way her gaze lingered longer than necessary as it found him.

He nodded a greeting and made his way to the bar. And she was there, with that look and a hand on his arm.

"Wot can Mac get for you?" she inquired with a look over her shoulder at the man behind the bar.

He picked up the Scots accent as Mac finally made his way to the end of bar.

Brodie nodded in that silent language of places like this— ale usually the first choice, as it was cheap and there was no doubt an ample supply in the back room.

A frothy brew in a tankard arrived, and he took a long drink as his gaze swept the pub for the worker Mr. Dooley had described who had seen the murderer. He found him across the smoke-filled room at a table playing a game of dice.

There for a bit of the drink after workin' on a London street, the day's work caked on the man's shirt with sleeves rolled back, coarse pants with suspenders and hair that had been plastered to his head with sweat and then dried.

He didn't approach him straight off, but watched him, the table, and the others gathered there. It appeared the man was having a run of luck as he shouted with laughter, then swept the coins he'd won into the palm of one hand. Enough for the next round.

Bets were made as more ale arrived, and the game began again.

Brodie stayed at the bar and ordered another, then struck up a conversation with the woman as she filled her tray with drinks, then returned a short while later with empty mugs.

"A bit of a '*stramash*' here the night before," he said to give the impression that he had been there, another face in the crowd, and was merely making a comment.

"Aye," she replied with an inviting smile.

Her name was Meara.

"Emptied the place, it did, and cut the evenin' short and me pay, when the police arrived." She threw a look of open invitation over her shoulder as she picked up another tray of ale.

"Got to make up for it tonight." She wound her way through the tables, picking up empty tankards along the way and delivering full ones, at the same time escaping just out of reach of a wandering hand.

She made her way back to the end of the bar.

"I heard a man got himself knifed?" Brodie added to the conversation as she sidled up beside him, fanning herself with a bar towel as Mac loaded her tray once more.

"That's what I heard and sent off to hospital," Meara replied. "It was that newspaper fella wot comes in regular, right Mac?"

Mac grunted. "Looking for information, stirrin' up the customers with stories about himself. It was a bloody mess out the sidewalk. The police carried 'im off in their van."

"Disgusting little man," Meara added as she picked up the filled tray.

"How is that?" Brodie asked.

She dispensed fresh tankards and returned.

"It's the way he has of puttin' his hands on a woman," she said, with a look at Mac as he wiped the bar and then went to greet a customer at the other end.

"Like he owns 'em just for the price of ale. Get my meanin'?"

He did. He'd seen it hundreds of times.

"I say who gets to put his hands on me, and not that slimy bugger," she added as she leaned in closer, the roundness of a breast pressed against his arm where he sat at the bar.

She was pretty and smelled of soap along with ale. In another place, another life, he might have taken her up on the obvious offer...in that *other* life.

"It's a pity that a man canna enjoy a drink. Did anyone see who attacked him?" he casually asked.

"It was when the man left. They were outside. Someone said that the newspaper fella said he was meeting someone here. Seems like it went bad."

And Mikaela had been the person he was to meet.

"If it's not one of the regulars, then it's the ones just returned from outta the docks," Meara commented. "Smellin' like it too."

There was that invitation again in her smile as she reached out and stroked his beard. "I like 'em clean, not smelling of swill or the bottom of a fishin' boat."

"We got other customers, Meara!" Mac reminded her from the other end of the bar.

She smiled again and picked up the tray of mugs filled with ale.

As she left to take the next round to those who waited, one of the players at dice table stood.

"I've enough to pay for one more, then I'm for home, gentlemen."

He made a grand gesture of pulling coins from his pocket, almost went over, then straightened himself.

"Meara, darlin', I've a need for one more, if you please."

Brodie left the bar taking the mug of ale with him as he approached the table. He took an empty chair.

Over the next hour, the dice changed hands several times as conversation and bets rounded the table.

The man called Fitch groaned as he lost.

"That was new shoes for me boy."

When the dice came back round, he bet again, rolled and won. He grinned.

"Now I won't have to listen to me missus complainin' about them shoes."

As the evening wore on, Brodie bet, lost as the dice and cup were passed round, and struck up the usual sort of conversation found at a table with those were who were regular patrons.

"There was a dust-up here the other night," he commented. "That newspaper man, accordin' to the word on the street."

Fitch nodded. "Not that anyone here thinks much of him, buyin' drinks, askin' his questions, then hearin' about it wrote up in the daily sometimes different than was told."

Such was Burke's reputation, according to Mikaela and others Brodie knew. The man was notorious for twisting a story about.

"Attacked just outside the other night, I heard." Brodie shook his head as if simply sharing what he had learned on the street.

Fitch tossed the dice, lost then passed the cup. "He had it comin', if you ask a lot of them here, but I wouldn't wish that on anyone."

"I heard ye saw it," Brodie shook the cup and tossed the dice down onto the table.

Fitch nodded. "Afterward, when the man was layin' there."

"And the one who done it was a rough sort, accordin' to wot I heard." Brodie passed the cup to the man on his left.

Fitch shrugged. "The man just stood there in his fine

clothes." He frowned. "Come to think on it now, that seemed outta place here, you know? Them that come here don't have such finery."

That was something that hadn't been in Dooley's report.

"And the bloke just stood over him for a few moments, lookin' satisfied instead of takin' off like most would have."

Fitch was thoughtful as he took the cup and shook it.

"It was the same look from me supervisor when we finish a section of roadwork by end of day. Satisfied over wot we done. It gave me a cold feelin'. Then he left and got into a coach down the way."

Fine clothes. And a coach. Two more pieces of information not in the report. It told Brodie more about the man who had attacked Burke.

"A private coach?" he commented then to draw more out of Fitch. "Not something ye see around here."

Fitch tossed the dice, won, and scooped up coins that had been bet against him. He shook his head as he set out his next bet.

"Not private. It had one of those metal plates on the back that the city gives to drivers."

A rented coach. Another piece that could be useful.

The game continued as the cup was passed round, the players changing from time to time as bets were won, then lost.

Stragglers wandered into the Old Bell, then thinned as the evening wore on. Brodie watched from the table over ale that he drank sparingly.

Meara arrived at the table, cleared empty mugs, and exchanged a new round.

"There's one for you," she commented with a jerk of her chin toward the bar.

"Tight-fisted," she spat out. "Pays only enough for the

drink with no thought to them that needs a few extra coins to pay the rent. As if he can't spare it. And he's got an evil eye."

Brodie looked past her to the man at the bar. He'd noticed him when he arrived, dressed in trousers with a black jumper beneath his coat, a billed cap pulled low.

The description that Fitch had given the police that night was there—compact body, thick-muscled at the shoulders, and the way he moved as if he might have just stepped off the boxing stage, wearing the fine clothes that didn't belong in that part of London.

Brodie continued to watch him as the dice rolled. A spare movement, ale that went untouched as he spoke with Mac. The slow looks around the pub, pausing then moving on, eventually resting on the man across from him who pushed back his chair.

"I'm for home," Fitch announced. "I've a bit more coin in my pockets than I started with." He smiled as he stood. "The missus will be glad to see me."

There was knowing laughter from the others at the table as Brodie continued to watch the man at the bar

"And here's one for you, Meara darlin'." Fitch tossed a coin onto her tray.

"You know that I love you," she replied. "If you weren't already married..."

It was the usual pub banter, yet Brodie noticed how the other man's gaze sharpened on Fitch.

It might have been no more than a reaction to that parting bit of conversation, but there was something more behind that narrowed gaze as Fitch pocketed his winnings then emptied that last mug of ale.

"I bid you good night, gentlemen." He made a sweeping

bow with good humor, then pulled his worn work coat from the chair back.

Brodie watched as Fitch left, the pub door snapping shut behind him, as the man at the bar in that fine coat took a drink, then set his almost full mug back on the bar, and followed.

Brodie signaled to Meara.

"Are you leavin' too?" she said with a disappointment she made no attempt to hide. "I was hopin' we might share some of the good stuff later," she said with a frown as he put on his jacket. "My room is just around the corner."

There was no attempt to disguise the invitation.

He tucked two coins into the bodice of her gown. He knew well enough how it worked, had seen it dozens of times.

"Mac doesn't need to know," he told her.

She balanced the tray as she leaned in and kissed his cheek.

"'Tis a shame. You must have someone waitin' home for you."

Brodie slipped his hand into his pocket as he left the pub, the steel of the revolver cool on his fingers.

There was a single streetlamp at the end of the street that framed Fitch as he made his way home and suddenly exposed the man who followed.

The attack was powerful, meant to drive Fitch to the cobbled stones. But Fitch worked on the streets, not behind a desk, and fought back, grunting as a blow fell. Then another.

Brodie ran, throwing his shoulder into the back of the man with that fine coat.

He swore and lost his hold.

"Get out of here!" he shouted at Fitch, curses cut off, the revolver jarred from his hand from blows meant not just to chase him off.

He fought back, driving the man up against the wall of a storefront, with that instinct from the streets.

The man was strong, persistent, grunting when Brodie landed a blow, then forcing him back with a punch and then a second one.

His boots slipped on the wet stones and he went down. The next blow came from the man's own boot to his ribs, driving the air from his lungs. He pushed back to his feet, the knife from his boot clenched in his fist. He slashed at the arm that would have brought the next blow.

His attacker cursed and clutched his arm. He glared at him, backed away, then turned and ran into the shadows, heading down the street in the opposite direction from which Fitch had fled.

Brodie winced at the pain that throbbed below his left eye, blood warm on his cheek.

He slowly straightened and cursed all over again at the pain in his ribs—likely broken and not the first time.

The man who had attacked him was experienced, not simply someone off the street. His clothes were not what those who frequented the Old Bell wore. And he had singled Fitch out.

He retrieved the revolver and slowly made his way to the high street, where he hoped to find a driver. Perhaps one foolish enough to be out after spending the last hours in a pub.

Four

MIKAELA, THE STRAND

I HAD BEEN TEMPTED to stay over the night at Sussex Square as it grew later.

However, there was information to add to my notes on the chalkboard. Admittedly, that could have waited until the following morning, however I hoped there might be some word at the office from Lily in Edinburgh.

Aunt Antonia's driver, Mr. Hastings, delivered me back to the office.

There was no telegram, no letter telling me when she might return, Mr. Cavendish informed me when I arrived.

"She's safe enough with Mr. Munro, miss. Not to worry."

Of course. And then there was Brodie. I had hoped that he might have returned with some word about what he had learned that day. Mr. Cavendish's response was the same in that regard.

"Not as yet, miss. You know how it is when he takes to the streets."

He had then added. "He wouldn't much care for you returning here alone for the night, so best take the hound up to the office with you."

So here I was, notes completed, a glass tumbler with a wee dram of Old Lodge whisky, and Rupert appearing as if he might have died on the rug before the coal stove, except for an occasional twitch and one eye that opened briefly as I moved about the office and added those notes from what I had learned.

I then went to my desk and stared at my typewriting machine, with a blank sheet of paper staring back at me as rain began. I inserted the paper, rolled it into place and began to type:

> *'It was a dark and storming night as Emma Fortestcue returned alone to the flat she now shared with police Inspector McKenzie.*
>
> *He had taken to the streets once more, familiar places after a troubled youth with things best left in the past, he told her when she had asked about them'*
>
> *Well past midnight, there was a stirring at the door. Startled, she looked up as...'*

Bloody hell! I thought, as Rupert was suddenly on his feet, charging toward the door, hair raised on his back as he let out that baying sound that only meant one thing. I retrieved the revolver from my bag and slowly approached as he continued to sound the alarm, placing himself between the door and me.

There was more stirring at the door, the lock turned, and the door slowly opened.

"Oh, bloody hell!" An understatement as I took in the man who leaned against the door opening, dried blood above his beard on his left cheek, holding himself with one arm wrapped about him as if he might break.

"I'd probably feel better if ye shot me," he said with a glance at the revolver in my hand. A bit of wry Scots humor that, I thought, as I laid the revolver aside, then returned and slipped an arm about him.

"Easy, lass."

It did seem pointless to ask if he was injured. He winced as he leaned heavily against me.

"And the other man?" I inquired at the sight of the dried stain on his coat sleeve as we slowly made our way across the office and he eased down into the chair at his desk.

"Yer concern is touching," he replied.

I ignored the sarcasm as I went into the adjacent room and filled a basin of water and returned with a towel.

That dark gaze narrowed, his cheek below bloodied, from a cut.

"I'd much prefer a shot of whisky."

"Of course," I replied, forcing back the alarm at the sight of him as I reminded myself that he was very much alive, sharp comments and all.

"Do ye know wot ye are doing?"

"For the most part," I replied. "Rupert survived his injuries some months ago without further harm."

"A bloody hound?" he replied, obviously in a great deal of pain that seemed far more than the bruise and cut on his face.

The 'bloody hound' sat nearby, the hair on his back still standing on end as he eyed Brodie suspiciously, as if attempting to decide whether or not he should attack.

"Do you want me to send for Mr. Brimley?"

The chemist and good friend had some experience previously attending various wounds, including my own. He had studied medicine at King's College and then set up his shop in one of the poorest parts of London, attending to those who needed care.

"Ye dinna need to contact him. It's but a scratch. Wot I do want is a good drink to help dull the pain."

"Mr. Brimley has cautioned about drinking when recovering from a wound," I reminded him. His response was quite colorful.

Since becoming part in our inquiry cases and our more personal relationship, I have learned to pick my battles.

"Do ye want me to pour it myself?" he commented, somewhat more civil.

I tossed the cloth into the bowl, went to the side table, and poured a small amount. I returned and handed it to him, then retrieved the cloth from the bowl of water.

"Should I prepare myself for a visit from the police with a body lying somewhere about London?" I inquired.

The cut had stopped bleeding somewhere along his travels back to the office. I wiped dried blood from his cheek surrounding the cut and then in his beard.

"This is going to be quite colorful." I announced.

When there was no wry comment, I looked up. He was staring past me to the chalkboard.

"Ye made more notes."

That dark gaze narrowed. "Southwark?"

He cursed again, this time in Gaelic. It was far more impressive than English, with that sound that needed no translation.

"Have ye lost the common sense God gave ye, woman? A man has been murdered, and ye take it upon yerself to go there *alone*?"

That little voice inside my head cautioned that he was obviously exhausted, wounded.

I calmly set the bowl and towel aside, as it did seem that he was not in imminent danger of expiring from the wound.

"I learned there is a woman in Southwark who may very well be Adele DeMille, after I found information at Burke's office," I explained. "It was on a laundry receipt dated just two days ago."

That dark gaze pinned me.

"Ye took it upon yerself to go there, without tellin' me first and waitin' so that I could go with ye?"

"Mr. Jarvis was not familiar with the area. It seemed that the time was better spent going to Sussex Square," I calmly explained. "I did want to speak with Aunt Antonia about that gold button." I didn't point out that if he had read all the notes, he would have noticed that particular one.

Brodie tossed back the last of the whisky.

"Wot about the button?"

"Buttons such as the one we found in St. John's Wood are usually requested by those who can afford them, including those in the military." I frowned as he held out his glass for another dram.

I poured and explained further. "Buttons of that quality are quite expensive and almost always have some emblem on the front, usually the family crest. It's a sign of..."

"Wealth and authority," he added.

"There was something else she explained that we had not noticed," I continued. "Such buttons are individually made to exact measurements and quality, not like wood or bone buttons."

Brodie took a sip, winced as he shifted in his chair, then took another longer drink. He was obviously in a great deal of pain that appeared to have nothing to do with the cut below his left eye.

"Go on."

I watched his expression and the way he held himself as I continued.

"There are usually embossed letters or a distinctive mark on the reverse of the button for the name of the person who made it, or possibly the person it was made for."

"Is a mark on the back of the button?"

"The letters R.M." I replied. "There are a number of custom tailor shops in London where we might be able to find out who that is."

I would have explained further if Rupert hadn't suddenly come to his feet once more and charged the door. Brodie winced again as he retrieved his revolver and pushed to his feet with some effort as the door opened.

"Ye might call the beast off!" the man who had once served with Brodie snarled. "Before I toss him over the railing."

That would have been a sight to see indeed, as Mr. Conner entered the office with that noticeable limp from an old injury and went to the side table and that bottle of Old Lodge whisky.

"It's bloody cold outside," he announced as he poured, tossed back the entire contents, then poured again and turned with a smile.

"Pretty as usual, Lady Forsythe." He looked from me to Brodie. "I'm not interrupting anything, am I?"

Brodie made a sound as he lowered himself back into the chair.

"I thought to bring you wot I learned tonight..." Mr. Conner commented. "You look like hell. Wot the devil happened?"

"It would seem there is more to it than the cut on yer cheek, with ye bent over like an old man."

"It is good to see ye as well," Brodie told him.

"Wot are ye hiding under yer coat?" Mr. Conner asked.

"A few bruises, no more."

Mr. Conner nodded. "Aye, I heard that before. Off with the coat."

"Ye are worse than an old woman!"

The 'woman' in the room chose not to take exception to that as Mr. Conner helped remove his coat.

"The shirt as well. I doubt there's anything Lady Forsythe has not seen before," he added with a grin.

Brodie glared at him.

The jumper he wore presented a different problem. It fit rather tight across his shoulders and chest and took some effort to remove as he winced and cursed.

My throat tightened at the sight of the large, dark bruise that spread across his ribs on his left side.

"Just as I thought," Mr. Conner announced. "Does it hurt here and here?" he asked as he poked around the bruise.

"Leave off!" Brodie told him. "I can take care of myself."

Mr. Conner looked over at me.

"Has he been coughin' or bringin' up any blood?"

"No," I replied as I stared at that bruise.

"That's a good sign. Some strong cloth will do... The ribs are broken—two, maybe more. He needs to be bound up so there's no further injury."

"I've had broken ribs before..."

Mr. Conner ignored him as I tried to think what we had in the way of cloth that might be used.

I did wish Mr. Brimley were there as I glanced at that gruesome bruise. At the moment, Brodie looked as if he would like to throw a blow at his friend as he held himself against the pain.

"A lady's corset would do."

It did seem as though Mr. Conner was enjoying this, as Brodie glared at him.

I went into the adjacent room that we shared and tore through the clothes in the wardrobe as well as the chest of drawers. Then turned to the bed and quickly removed the sheet.

Mr. Conner stared at me with some amusement as I returned with the sheet.

"I do not wear a corset," I informed him.

"I thought not. No offense, Lady Forsythe. We'll need that cut into strips to bind him with."

I proceeded to cut then tear the sheet into long strips several inches wide.

Much cursing followed from Brodie and then silence, as he sat on the chair and Mr. Conner bound him about his ribs.

"There," Mr. Conner declared, standing back to inspect his work. "That should do for a while."

Brodie shifted in the chair. "Ye might explain wot ye learned,"

"Of course." He looked over at me. "Another dram, if ye please, Lady Forsythe."

He waited until I had poured more whisky.

"I managed to visit four pubs Burke has been known to frequent. The man did get around."

He downed the whisky and held out his glass once again.

"With this leg of mine, it required the services of a cabman, as I canna walk as far as I used to," he continued. "Ye owe me sixpence," he told Brodie, then took a long sip of whisky.

"The first two pubs, he hadn't been around for a while.

But he had been to the third one before visitin' the Old Bell on the night he was killed.

"There was somethin' else. It seems there was another man askin' about him."

He provided the description he'd been given, and I saw something shift in Brodie's expression. Mr. Conner saw it as well.

"Perhaps the man ye encountered tonight?" he suggested. Brodie nodded. "Aye."

"There's more. The man was recognized by a man at the bar who used to frequent the sports club in Germantown."

The sports club was well-known across London. I had been there several times and Lily as well, as they now had a women's exercise program, as well as other sports training.

I had insisted that she take formal lessons in handling a sword, admittedly not the usual interest for a young lady. However, I could hardly argue the matter, and lessons did seem necessary for the safety of everyone at Sussex Square. As it turned out, she was quite talented.

"It could be useful to see what the owner knows about the man," Mr. Conner suggested. "I'm for my own bed. It's been a long time since I patrolled the streets and made inquiries. And this knee of mine is stiffening up. By the way," he added. "Ye look like the devil, and ye shouldn't move around with those ribs busted."

"Ye are not my mother, nor my wife."

However, I was much in agreement, and amid much protest, Mr. Conner assisted in removing Brodie from the outer office to the adjoining bed chamber.

Though not without a good measure of curses, mostly in the language they both understood.

Then as he turned to leave, "That will be another sixpence

for assisting an invalid," he remarked, good-natured in spite of the fact that it was two o'clock in the morning and he obviously had some discomfort of his own as well as being tired.

I thanked him for his 'assistance.'

"It will be worse the next couple of days," he warned. "I know from experience. The challenge is to keep him quiet. Good luck with that."

He grinned as he departed.

I looked over at Brodie, eyes closed, trussed up with that bandage, but hardly asleep.

"The man has a devious nature," he commented, exhaustion in his voice.

"You should be grateful to him."

"It would encourage him, though he does seem to think highly of ye." He winced. "It might have to do with the fact that he knows yer right handy with the revolver."

I had no experience with broken ribs and could only imagine the pain Mr. Conner had described.

I set the lock in the office door and put more coal on fire in the firebox, then returned to the bedchamber. With a thought to sleeping in the outer office, so not to disturb him, I grabbed the extra blanket folded at the foot of the bed.

I felt that dark gaze on me.

"I would have ye sleep here, lass," he said.

"You're injured. I don't want to cause any difficulty."

I could have sworn he laughed, a low sound in his throat, then swore and cursed again.

"There's more the difficulty if someone should come through the office door and I need to protect ye."

It was an old argument.

I said nothing as I returned the blanket, then undressed and slipped into the bed on his other side.

He shifted to make more room, and I heard the sudden breath he took at the pain it caused. He slowly breathed out as he wrapped his arm around me and pulled me close.

"Your ribs?" I cautioned.

"This is all I need."

I felt the bristly touch of his beard on the back of my shoulder as he kissed me there.

"Go to sleep, lass."

Five

BRODIE SAT in the chair at his desk as he read the notes I'd made from the day before.

Mr. Conner had returned a short while earlier and sat across from him.

"I've seen worse," he commented as he looked across at Brodie. "The color purple suits ye. There will be a scar from the cut, but the ladies are drawn to that," he added, with a look over at me, amusement in his eyes.

"What is the plan for today?" he then asked.

It had been a restless night. Brodie had hardly slept, shifting from one side to the other, then back again. I had risen early with the hope he might get more sleep. He had then appeared at the adjoining door with a bruised expression and a single word as he slowly made his way to the desk.

"Coffee."

I had set a fresh pot on the stove when I first rose that morning. I poured a cup and handed it to him.

My skills in that regard had improved admirably. Or

perhaps not, as he grimaced, cursed, then struggled to swallow, and looked at me with narrowed eye.

"Ye could stand a spoon in it."

I took it as a compliment.

Mr. Conner had not complained when he arrived.

"Aye, strong. Just the way I like it," he said when I poured a cup for him as well.

"What about the cabman Fitch spoke of?" he asked now. "There could be something there if he remembers where he delivered the man."

Brodie nodded. "And perhaps a visit to Germantown. The man who attacked me last night might be known at the gymnasium. The blows he threw were not the sort learned on the street."

"So it would seem." Mr. Conner nodded.

"The man was sent by someone. The question is, who might that be and for what reason?

"Burke made his reputation on sordid, sensational articles that he wrote for the newspaper. It didn't seem to matter whether the subject was someone in Parliament or a member of the peerage. Any one of them might have taken exception to something he wrote."

Brodie shook his head. "He's insulted dozens of persons across London, and nothing has come of it before." He frowned. "There's more to this, and it has to do with the name on that note he gave Mikaela."

"There is also the address in Southwark," I pointed out. "It could be important."

Brodie explained the receipt that I had found. Mr. Conner nodded.

"Southwark is not a place where you should go."

If there was anything worse than one badly bruised Scot

who'd had little sleep the night before, it was another overbearing Scot, in spite of the smile and the twinkle in his eyes.

"But ye have no doubt heard that before."

"I suppose my place would be here brewing coffee and keeping my notes," I replied.

Brodie angled a look at me that spoke clearly about my efforts at making coffee or anything else that might require skill in a kitchen. I chose to ignore him and his bruises.

"There are other things for a woman to see to," Mr. Conner commented with a look across at Brodie.

"It would seem that 'other things' are now sharply curtailed due to the events of last evening," I replied.

"Did I say something to offend?" Mr. Conner commented.

"Ye have been warned," Brodie told him.

"I apologize if I offended, Lady Forsythe," Mr. Conner added.

"Apology accepted. However, you may make your own coffee."

Brodie laughed, winced, then cursed at the pain it caused.

It was decided over a second pot of coffee that Mr. Conner took it upon himself to set on the stove, that he would make inquiries about the coachman who aided the murderer's escape the night Burke was killed.

I would call on Herr Schmidt at the sports club in Germantown to see what might be learned about the man who was seen the night Burke was murdered and had attacked Brodie the night before.

"Ye'll not go alone," Brodie told me after Mr. Conner left.

"I could easily go to Germantown myself so that you might rest. I do know Herr Schmidt," I pointed out, that dark gaze watching me.

"I can take the hound with me," I added. "Then you would

be here when Mr. Conner returns with any information about the driver."

That dark gaze narrowed as he finished buttoning his shirt. I had my answer.

"Very well," I continued. "However, you have only yourself to blame if you injure yourself further."

It took considerably more effort to pull on his coat.

I retrieved my coat as well as my travel bag, and we left the office. He relented as far as taking the lift down to the street, which he had refused in the past.

Contrary to something I had once read, it did seem that it was possible to teach an old dog new tricks. It was tempting to comment on that, though I did not. It was undoubtedly best not to 'poke the *bear*,' or in this case an injured *bear*.

I had asked Mr. Cavendish to secure a driver before leaving the office. Mr. Jarvis sat atop his coach when we arrived at the sidewalk. He swung down and opened the coach door.

"Where will it be?"

Brodie gave him the destination in Germantown, and I climbed into the coach. He followed and slowly eased down onto the seat opposite.

I felt that dark gaze watching me as Mr. Jarvis eased the coach into midmorning traffic.

"*Other things?*" Brodie commented, referring to that earlier conversation with Mr. Conner about a woman's place.

"Was that a complaint?"

I knew perfectly well what he referred to and refused to dignify that with an answer.

"It does look as if the rain might hold off a while longer," I replied instead as I stared out the coach window.

He could be such a devil.

It was late morning by the time we reached the sports club.

Germantown was a community of immigrants who had arrived in London over the past several years, along with others. The conversations on the street a blend of English, their native languages, and others from across Europe.

Some had returned to their home countries, but the majority remained and established shops, taverns, or worked for others in the growing community.

Herr Schmidt had established the sports club at the edge of Germantown. His clientele came from across London and included the titled with a growing fascination in various athletic sports, as well ladies' exercise classes.

As for my own interests, he had been most amused at my inquiries regarding fencing.

"It is not a discipline for ladies," he informed me at the time.

Not to be put off, I had returned several days later with a rapier from the Sword room at Sussex Square and politely informed him that I had previous instruction.

"Very well, show me what you have learned," he said with some amusement as he led me onto the floor of the gymnasium where a wooden training target hung by a chain suspended from the ceiling.

I had learned several maneuvers at those lessons in Paris, including the technique for parry, then the moves against an opponent, deflection when attacked, and countermoves.

After several moves, then a final strike against the target, Herr Schmidt had shouted 'halt' to end the exercise.

"It is not fitting for a woman to use such a weapon," he had grumbled more than once. "I would not allow it for my wife. It would be too dangerous. But I know of a man who may be able to provide lessons."

I had attended those lessons with Monsieur Montclair for

over a year and learned considerably more. In that time, I had achieved a certain respect from the stout German, and he had since assisted us with a previous inquiry case.

When we arrived, an attendant at the front counter found Herr Schmidt out on the main floor of the gymnasium.

Not merely the owner of the gymnasium but also a trainer, he had been working with one of the participants for a boxing contest that was to be held at the week's end.

He wore trousers, bare-chested, that long moustache at either side of thick jowls, as he wiped sweat from his face and neck, and made no apology for his appearance.

"Lady Forsythe," he said in greeting. "You are the only woman not insulted by such a sight."

He then looked over at Brodie, his gaze narrowing at the sight of the purplish bruise and cut below his eye.

"And the other one who gave you that, Herr Brodie?" he inquired.

"It is about that we need to speak with ye," he replied.

Herr Schmidt nodded, and we followed him to the room that served as an office. He retrieved a shirt, buttoned it across that barrel chest, the sleeves loosely rolled back. He poured a glass and offered it to Brodie.

"Schnapps," he said. "It will ease the pain. My cousin sends it to me by the case. The English do not know how to make it."

"Thank ye, but no," Brodie replied.

Herr Schmidt nodded and took a long drink.

"Now, tell me, what is it that has brought you here?"

Brodie explained about the attack at the Old Bell, saying only that we were making inquiries in the matter for the police. He didn't mention Burke's name.

Herr Schmidt nodded over his glass. "I heard of this. It can be dangerous to go to a pub." A grin appeared under that silver moustache. "But a bit of excitement is always good. Yes?"

"The attacker was seen that night." Brodie gave him the description that Fitch had provided. "I had an encounter with him as well."

Herr Schmidt nodded. "And this man walked away? That is not what I have heard about you."

"In a manner of speaking. He has a knife wound now."

I looked over at him with some surprise. He had not mentioned that part of the encounter.

Herr Schmidt nodded. "Perhaps he has simply gone off somewhere and bled to death." He was thoughtful and set his glass on the top of the desk. "I know of this man. He is not German. He is Austrian, highly skilled with his fists...as you have experienced. He is, how do you say..." He searched for the word in English. "An assassin. He is well paid by those who can afford his time, and he takes great pleasure in causing pain." That sharp gaze met Brodie's across the desk.

"He is from Linz, though he calls no country home. It is said that he fought his way out of the iron ore mines there, though the story changes depending on who is telling it.

"I've heard rumors about him," he continued. "It is unknown what you can believe. Only the bodies know, eh? And they don't speak."

He gave Brodie a long look, then reached for his glass once more and poured more Schnapps.

"What is known is that he lives well and dresses as you have described him. You are fortunate to have survived the encounter."

"The man's name?" Bodie replied.

"He calls himself Steiner. It means *from stone*. And he is that."

"I need to know whom he works for."

"As I said, those who can afford to pay his fee. I mean no offense, Lady Forsythe, but he is the sort of man who will be found in the company of those with titles, wealth, and power. More than that," he shrugged. "I do not know. Nor do I want to know.

"I have my family, and this place that I have worked hard for. A man like Steiner does not value anything other than what another man will pay him, although it is said that he has a particular...appetite for a beautiful woman." He looked over at me.

"If Steiner is the man Herr Brodie is looking for, you must be careful Lady Forsythe. I would not want anything to happen to you. Do you still carry a weapon?"

Brodie winced as the coach lurched across uneven pavement in the roadway as we left the gymnasium.

Burke murdered. That note he had given me. Brodie attacked after leaving the Old Bell. And now to learn the man who had attacked him was a known assassin.

"What has this to do with Burke and that note?" I said, trying to make sense of it all.

"Ye said often enough that the man would sell his soul for a story for the newspaper, and he built his reputation on the crime and scandal sheets for the Times," Brodie commented.

"The better question would be, wot is it about a story that was worth his life?"

It made sense. But what did that have to do with me?

Brodie braced himself as the coach lurched again, then slowly let out the breath he was holding.

After leaving the gymnasium, I had suggested that he return to the office to await word from Mr. Conner, while I continued on with the hope of learning something about that gold button.

He had given me 'that look.'

Savile Row was in Mayfair. It was a part of London I knew well, with tailor shops for gentlemen, and included one with a royal warrant, Henry Poole & Company, which had provided military tailoring for officers for decades, from before the Battle of Waterloo. Along with one dress uniform of a Montgomery cousin that was presently in the sword room at Sussex Square.

The foyer of Henry Poole & Co. of London was tastefully furnished and might have been the entrance to any private residence at St. James's or Portman Square, with thick carpet, a mahogany desk, an attendant who greeted us, and a long hallway that extended to the back of the shop, no doubt with fitting rooms and work areas.

"Lady Forsythe," the young man acknowledged when I gave my name, then slanted more than one curious glance at Brodie, the bruise below his eye now a glorious shade of purple.

Brodie explained the reason we were there, after finding an unusual button and the need to determine who it might belong to.

"Of course," the young man replied, somewhat hesitant and with another glance at Brodie.

"I will inform our concierge."

"Bloody hell," Brodie commented as the young man departed. "Wot the devil is a concierge?"

With experience limited to ladies' dress shops, it was safe to assume it was much the same in a men's shop, particularly one that provided formal wear and waistcoats to gentlemen across London that included members of the royal family.

"It would perhaps be the manager of the shop," I ventured to guess as the man returned and introduced a formally dressed man, Mr. Hendley.

He stared at Brodie for a moment, then cleared his throat.

"How may I assist you?"

Brodie explained the reason for our visit once more, and we were escorted into a private office that resembled a small sitting room, furnished with a mahogany desk and chairs.

"May I see the item?"

I retrieved the button and handed it across the desk. Mr. Hendley laid it on a white linen cloth, then took out a looking glass and examined the button.

"It is finely made. Real gold, I would say, not plated, with a somewhat unusual insignia."

"Do you recognize it?" I inquired.

"Not precisely." He looked up. "Yet, there are many family crests and marks that our clients request."

He removed a book from one of the desk drawers. It was bound in leather and embossed across the front with the name of the company. It appeared to be a catalogue of crests and emblems. He scanned the first page, then a handful more. He shook his head.

"We do keep a reference for all our work. That crest is not among them." He was thoughtful. "It does seem to be the style that might be used by a private gentlemen's club.

"There are several, as well as fraternal orders, religious symbols, insignias that have a personal meaning. However, this does not appear to have been made by our people."

It was disappointing, still it was possible that the button

had been made in one of the other shops. We inquired at two more shops nearby and received the same answer.

"It is possible the button was made elsewhere, perhaps Paris or another city. It does seem that Adele DeMille entertained a variety of *'guests.'*"

We entered the next shop, Gieves & Hawkes, a well-known clothier for members of Parliament and other gentlemen.

As with the other shops we had called upon, it was furnished as one might expect in a fine home, with a front counter where we were greeted by an older man in a finely made suit. And as before, Brodie explained the reason for our visit.

"Of course," he replied. "Please wait here."

Another man appeared and introduced himself with a polite smile as Mr. Soames.

I showed him the gold button which he examined under a glass, also as before, his assistant moving closer for a look as well.

"Most impressive work, a wolf's head. The insignia is somewhat unusual, perhaps for a member of a private club." He turned it over and noted the letters on the reverse, usually etched by the craftsman who had made them.

"R.M. The letters do not mean anything to me, certainly not one of our clients."

His assistant had moved closer and peered over his shoulder. I was about to ask if he recognized it, when he turned and mumbled something about woolen cloth that needed to be attended to.

He quickly moved toward the back of the shop, which seemed somewhat unusual. He made a quick glance back over his shoulder that seemed suspicious. Brodie had seen it as well.

I rounded the counter to Mr. Soames's protest and ran through the shop after his assistant, as Brodie turned and left through the main entrance.

The door at the back of the shop slowly closed as I ran past startled workers at cutting tables.

I followed out that door and into the alleyway and glanced in both directions. He seemed to have disappeared.

Had he recognized the insignia on the button? Was it possible that he had made the button without the owner's knowledge? If so, why had he fled, and where had he gone?

Brodie had said more than once that in order to know a person's thoughts, you had to think as they would. If I were attempting to flee a situation, where would I go?

The alleyway passed along behind other shops on Savile Row, while the opposite end opened onto a street that adjoined Regent Street just beyond.

He might have stepped into any one of those shops, odd as it would have seemed to those inside. Or he might very well have fled toward the street and escaped into the traffic of coaches and trams.

I ran to the back door of the next shop over. The door was locked. No help there. I then ran to the next one, greeted by startled workers who looked up. No one had entered the shop before me. Nor at the two shops beyond. The little man with those thick spectacles had disappeared.

"Bloody hell."

I returned to the shop where we had encountered him. According to the shop owner his name was Louis Jardine. He had been employed by the shop a little more than a year. He was highly skilled, a valued member of their staff, and there had never been any issue with his service.

He was quite clear that he didn't recognize the image on the front of the button as having been made in his shop.

"What would the image of a wolf represent?" I then asked.

"In some cultures, it has been known to represent power."

Louis Jardine had come to the owner of the shop with excellent recommendations. He lived in a flat at Portman Square, which had surprised Mr. Soames. While there were areas surrounding where working families lived, the Square was noted for flats and entire apartments held by professional people. The rents would be far more than a clerk in a men's shop could afford.

Mr. Jardine had explained that he had money from another source. The shop owner assumed that it was an inheritance.

I thanked him and went in search of Brodie. I found him at the end of Savile Row, at the corner of that cross street.

I suspect that pursuing someone afoot was not usually recommended for someone with broken ribs. He leaned against the side of a building, one arm wrapped about himself, obviously in great pain.

"I believe a visit from Mr. Brimley is in order."

"There is no need!" he insisted with a grimace of pain.

Yes, well...

"I learned something that could be important," I explained as a diversion, as we slowly returned to where Mr. Jarvis waited with the coach.

"The clerk's name and a possible meaning of that image on the button."

As we returned to the coach, I could only imagine that we must look quite odd, Brodie slowly taking each step, as if he'd had far too much to drink.

Theodolphus Burke, scandalmonger that he was, would

have been delighted to write about it in the next issue of the Times:

> *"Lady Mikaela Forsythe, who calls herself an author and well-travelled adventuress, was seen at Savile Row, assisting former Police Inspector Angus Brodie, obviously well into his drink, who could barely walk. A new murder case, perhaps?"*

"I'VE SEEN WORSE," Mr. Brimley commented as he inspected the cut below Brodie's eye much to the patient's irritation.

He had arrived earlier, after I placed a call to his shop.

"Fortunate the bone there is not broken. You have a hard head."

I could have made a comment to that, however, now was probably not the moment for that, with Brodie bound up around his ribs once more and still in a great deal of pain.

"And the ribs? Very likely two or three cracked," Mr. Brimley continued.

He had loosened the wrap and inspected the bruise over Brodie's ribs that was now the size of a grapefruit.

"But they all seem to be intact, though you might have torn the muscle there. That could also account for the pain. The syrup I've provided will give relief for a while." He looked over at me.

"Every eight hours will help with the pain, if you can persuade him to take it."

Laudanum. Brodie had refused to take any.

"I've seen wot it does to a man," he had replied.

Mr. Brimley looked at me as he prepared to leave.

"There will be considerable pain over the next several days. I wish you luck, Miss Forsythe."

"I'll see that he behaves himself," Mr. Conner assured him.

He had returned shortly after we arrived back at the office.

He was able to learn the name of the London company that had provided coach service near the Old Bell tavern the night Burke was murdered.

As he told us what he had learned, he went to the chalkboard and looked at the notes I added the previous evening.

"The man I spoke with pulled the record from that night. The customer paid an extra fare for the amount of time to take him to the pub, and then waited until he was ready to leave."

"Were ye able to learn the name of the driver?" Brodie replied as I handed him a glass with a dram of Old Lodge whisky.

Perhaps not the best 'medicine,' yet one that he accepted and quickly downed.

"A man by the name of Morse," Mr. Conner replied, "who lives in a tenement near Covent Garden. He's out and about now on his daily route, but he returns to the yard with his rig by early evening. I'll be there to ask him a few questions."

Brodie had made a telephone call to Inspector Dooley at the Yard when we first returned to the office, to let him know what we had learned that morning.

In that same conversation, Mr. Dooley shared there had been several inquiries from newspapers about the 'incident' at the Old Bell, with rumors and speculation regarding Burke's condition and whereabouts.

He had forestalled any comment for now, but then

cautioned that the time would come very soon when a statement would have to be made.

I thought it more than a little ironic that Burke was now the subject of both rumor and speculation.

In that same conversation, Brodie had informed Mr. Dooley that we were pursuing additional information regarding possible motives for the attack.

"Portman Square?" Mr. Conner commented as he read the entries I had made on the chalkboard after that telephone conversation ended.

"Not where ye might think to find a common tailor."

Brodie agreed. "Aye, and it was obvious that he recognized the image on that button. He may even know the customer it was made for, who was obviously at the residence in St. John's Wood."

"A gold button worth a year's wages for any other man. And just one button. I've seen the toffs over the years dressed in their finery with no thought to the man who made those fine clothes."

It was not the first time that I was made aware of the disparity between the class that I had been born into and the one both Mr. Conner and Brodie lived in.

"No offense, Miss Forsythe," he added.

Brodie's dark gaze met mine.

Neither of us had chosen the circumstances we had been born into. And yet, here we were.

My partnership with Brodie in our inquiry cases, as well as our personal relationship, was somewhat unusual, and it was not the first time I was aware of the difference between our classes.

Yet, as I had informed him from the beginning of our personal relationship when he had pointed out that we came from different places, I saw a man who had fought his way out of poverty on the streets of Edinburgh and London and made something of himself. Someone with more dignity and purpose than any man I had known.

For his part, he didn't attempt to change me, but had accepted me for who I was. Admittedly, with my own shortcomings, along with a somewhat stubborn nature, as he often reminded me. And something that was important to me—he was someone I could trust.

It was just past midday when Mr. Conner departed, to hopefully find the coachman who had taken a fare at the Old Bell from a man who fit the description of the same one who had attacked Brodie.

I had made notes in my notebook as well and now tucked it into my bag. I had added coal to the stove, then looked up as Brodie went to the coat stand. It took some effort as he pulled on the coat once more.

"You should stay and rest," I reminded him as I then went to retrieve my own coat, as a light rain had begun. "I'm perfectly capable of going to Portman Square to determine if Jardine went there after he disappeared. And you are in a great deal of pain."

"Aye, ye are capable."

There was that look in that dark gaze as he took my coat from the stand and then held it for me in spite of the pain.

"But the ribs will hurt whether I'm here or out and about," he replied.

And when I would have objected further...

"Are ye goin' to just stand there blatherin' about it?"

I slowly counted to ten, something I had learned in dealing with a temperamental man who was accustomed to having his own way in things.

'*Pick your battles,*' that inner voice whispered.

I thrust one arm into the sleeve of my coat, then the other, and left him to secure the office, as he bent with some effort to secure the lock to the office.

Mr. Jarvis had just delivered a fare on the Strand and swung his coach about.

Brodie gave him the address for Portman Square, and we climbed aboard, Brodie somewhat slower than usual as he took the seat across.

Portman Square was a pocket of middle-class residences that had emerged very near Regent Street, with the City of London's efforts at improving housing in areas of poverty.

The Square was an example of former tenements that had been repaired, remodeled, and then made available to professional persons who worked at offices, and those with up-scale businesses such as those at Savile Row and Bond Street.

As Mr. Conner had commented, however, while it was not on an equal with Mayfair, Kensington, or St. James's by any means, it was an address that seemed far beyond the means of a tailor's assistant.

Number 4 Portman Square was one of several apartments that fronted onto Old Bond Street, very near Regent Street, where one might find a cab or coach that could take him to Savile Row.

The question was, how might a tailor's assistant be able to afford a daily driver to take him to work there? An inheritance as his employer assumed?

There was a great deal about Mr. Jardine that simply did not make sense. Not the least was his reaction upon seeing that gold button.

We made the ride in a timely manner. Brodie asked Mr. Jarvis to wait as we stepped down to the street.

The contrast from the stark poverty in old tenements to the apartments at Old Bond Street, only a half dozen blocks apart, was startling.

We easily found the apartment building at #4 Portman Square and entered the foyer. According to the information his employer had, Louis Jardine lived in apartment 4-E.

I rang the service bell at the entrance, and a woman appeared who informed us that she was the matron of the building.

She was acquainted with Mr. Jardine, a quiet man who worked for a tailor. His rent was always paid on time, and she frequently saw him leaving of a morning, including earlier that same day. He then usually returned early in the evening after work. He had not yet returned today.

"I would know if he had," she insisted. She then proceeded to explain that he frequently forgot his key to his apartment and needed to use her key to get in. She shook her head.

"Absent-minded, you see. But an excellent craftsman. He made the medallion that I carry on my set of keys."

She had shown it to us, a delicate rose made of nickel plate. The detail was remarkable. He was obviously highly skilled.

"Would you care to leave a message?" she inquired. "I will see that he gets it."

Brodie replied with the excuse that he would call on Mr. Jardine at the tailor's shop.

"We might search his flat," I commented as we returned to the coach. "There might be something there that could explain the reason he left from the shop."

He glanced back at the building.

"But the woman would be at our heels the entire time, then callin' the police. We can return later."

I caught a glimpse of the woman we had spoken to at a window, the drape hastily dropped back into place.

It was late afternoon as we returned to the office on the Strand.

Mr. Jardine had not returned to the shop at Savile Row, Mr. Soames informed in a conversation by telephone.

He insisted that it was not like the man, who previously worked seven days a week when necessary to meet the schedule for a client who was expecting a special order. Punctual, loyal, a dedicated craftsman, it seemed. Who had apparently disappeared.

Two drams of whisky that had dulled the pain earlier had long since worn off, and Brodie shifted uncomfortably in the chair at his desk.

I made a couple of suggestions that might ease the pain, including the laudanum Mr. Brimley had provided. He shook his head.

"A dram of yer great aunt's whisky will do."

Spoken like a Scot. I poured a glass, then went down to the landing at the street and asked Mr. Cavendish to bring supper from the Public House. He inquired about Brodie's injuries.

"He's not one to take to bein' laid up."

"No, he is not," I replied.

I returned to the office as he set off across the Strand. The man in question had poured himself another dram of my great aunt's whisky and sat in his chair at the desk, his head against the chair back, eyes closed.

The pain was there, although dulled, no doubt somewhat from that first drink. He had not touched the laudanum that sat exactly where Mr. Brimley had left it before he departed earlier.

Bloody stubborn Scot, I thought. Though not without sympathy. While I had never broken any ribs, I had taken more than one tumble from one of my great aunt's horses that she raced at Ascot years before.

There is that moment when one has been unseated unceremoniously, dropped to the ground, and cannot catch one's breath. That particular incident had played itself over on one of my travels, though I had become somewhat more accomplished in my horsemanship skills by then.

I had discovered on a trek across the Sahara, however, that desert sand is no more forgiving than the track at Ascot. I had recovered from both, but not without substantial bruises.

The pain in both instances was gone in a matter of days, but not without the occasional reminder that I had been quite foolish. Not that it stopped me. In the years since, I had become quite accomplished at riding a horse. But the memory was still there.

Brodie's encounter was hardly a tumble from the back of a horse. He had suffered substantial injury with cracked ribs and the constant reminder of them with every move he made. It was there in the lines around his eyes and about his mouth.

"Not a word when I ask ye for another dram," he said now, without so much as cracking open an eye.

"Not a word," I replied as I bent over and gently kissed him.

"I prefer that to laudanum," he replied, still without opening an eye. "Perhaps even yer great aunt's whisky."

"I will remind you of that later."

He eventually stirred when Mr. Cavendish arrived, by way of the lift, with supper from the Public House.

"You might try ice for the pain," he suggested after taking a look at Brodie.

"Ye speak from experience?" Brodie inquired as I set our supper out on his desk.

Mr. Cavendish grinned. "There weren't no use for ice at the time. Me legs were already gone, cut clean off when the cargo shifted and trapped me under. Beg pardon, miss.

"Old Benny, who shipped over with us, said they were still there when they hoisted that crate from the deck," he continued. "Even now, I would swear I can feel me toes wigglin' about, and I don't have any. Me bride says it's me imagination. But it happens whenever the woman comes near."

For the first time since he'd been attacked, I caught the faint smile at one corner of Brodie's mouth. Toes. A most amusing tale.

It did seem that he fared no worse the second night after the attack, even though he moved about in the bed, unable to get comfortable, then eventually rose with a curse and went out into the adjacent office.

I joined him, unable to sleep as well, ignored his comment as I set the coffee pot on the stove, and poured him a dram of my great aunt's *tonic*.

I then returned to the adjoining chamber and dressed for the day. Afterward, I sat at my desk and went through the notes I'd made in my notebook.

It was barely light through the windows when the service bell on the landing broke the silence and rang persistently.

Inspector Dooley appeared at the door. He frowned, with a look over at Brodie, but made no comment about the bruise below his eye.

Brodie had updated him on the latest developments the previous evening, including our visit to Portman Square, only to find that Mr. Jardine had not returned there nor to the shop on Savile Row.

"Come along then," he said with a frown. "From the description you provided, it would seem that we've found the tailor."

We rode with Mr. Dooley to the London Docks in a coach provided by the Yard.

A handful of constables were gathered there, along with a police van. It quickly became apparent what they had gathered round.

Inspector Dooley nodded to one of them. "Mr. Brodie and Miss Forsythe are here on my authority," he told the constable, who stepped aside.

I had seen bodies before, admittedly an unfortunate part of our inquiry cases. In particular, the body of my sister's maid, which had been pulled from the Thames, cruelly murdered in my sister's disappearance.

I had asked Brodie then if one ever got used to such things. His silence in response was my answer, and I felt it now as I stared down at the body at the wharf and realized that I would never become used to it.

It was shocking, and at the same time enormously sad, that a human being would be reduced to nothing more than a bit of flotsam or garbage, thrown into a river to be gotten rid of.

Some were never found, while others often washed up against the pilings or floated among the dockside vessels, as if the person the body had once been was determined that others might know of their tragic end.

A day did not pass without another one washing up after suffering some misfortune—those who left taverns and were assaulted for a meager coin, a prostitute who had taken the company of the wrong person, most of them nameless and buried in a pauper's grave after being retrieved from the water.

The body that lay at the dock had a name, or at least had at one time—Louis Jardine, the tailor's assistant, whom we had hoped to speak with regarding that gold button.

I took a sudden deep breath as I stared down at the body with a combination of surprise and horror.

Brodie was there as he stepped between me and that ghastly sight, blocking my view of Jardine's body, bloated and battered from being tossed against the pilings with the incoming tide.

"Go back to the coach," he said gently. "There's no need for ye to be here."

"I'm quite all right," I insisted as I took another deep breath and remained as Mr. Dooley commented.

"There's a good deal of bruising about the torso and head," he pointed out. "The body hasn't been in the water that long. It would seem that someone had a go at him before he was dropped into the river. The lads went through his pockets," he added. "They were empty. It would seem to be the usual robbery."

Brodie crouched down beside the body in spite of the pain it brought.

"So it would seem," he commented as he inspected the injuries, then slowly stood once more.

"It's the tailor's assistant, but that is only for ye to know," he told Mr. Dooley. "I ask that no information be released to the newspapers yet."

Inspector Dooley grimly nodded. "What about Burke's body?"

"Nor about Burke. If whoever did this is curious, it might draw them out when there is nothing reported in the newspapers.

"There is more to this than another body of someone who had too much to drink, then washed up in the river."

And a woman who had entertained gentlemen, I thought, remembering where that button was found, and now she had apparently disappeared.

How was it all connected? What had Burke been pursuing when he was killed? What did it have to do with Adele DeMille? Or myself, for that matter, with that note he had given me, considering our somewhat contentious past?

"I'll do what I can," Mr. Dooley replied. "But there are those that will be poking around with the rumors that are already out on the street."

Chief Inspector Abberline.

Of course, I thought. Never let an opportunity that might improve one's position to pass by.

Abberline had thwarted our inquiries in the past. Though he was presently stationed at the Bow Street station, he did have a way of inserting himself into situations that might benefit him. And he had no doubt heard of the attack on Burke at the Old Bell.

"I understand," Brodie replied.

We waited in the coach as Mr. Dooley gave instructions to the constables who had found Jardine. He then returned to the coach as well.

"Let me know if you have any information that could be important," he said in parting.

"And I will do the same."

A look passed between them.

We took the lift up to the office. I poured coffee that had cooled considerably, then went to the chalkboard. I studied the most recent notes I'd made.

That insignia on that gold button could be important if we knew what it meant.

There was no word yet from Mr. Conner with his efforts to find the cabman who had driven the coach away from the Old Bell the night Burke was murdered. And then, there was the woman at the residence at St. John's Wood.

How was she connected to this, and why had Burke given me that note with her name on it?

Brodie studied the board as well. He'd had little sleep the night before. It showed in the faint lines at his eyes.

"I want to go to Southwark where that laundry order of lady's clothes was delivered. It could be important, particularly if she is there. I could be there and back within a few hours."

"And if there is someone there other than the woman?"

I had thought of that as well.

"I will take Rupert with me should there be any difficulty, and I will have the revolver with me," I pointed out.

There were few men who stood over me, given my height. However, that included the man who stood beside me.

"Aye, but ye'll not go alone. And I dinna mean the hound."

Seven

EVEN THOUGH IT was still the middle of the night for some, there was no sleep for either of us after we returned to the office. Instead, we went back over everything we had learned since that night when Burke was murdered.

I hoped that we might find some answers at that address in Southwark where those items on that laundry order had been delivered. Items obviously for a woman. Still, that raised even more questions.

Why Southwark? And who was the woman? Adele DeMille? If so, what was the connection to Burke of a woman who had once entertained men at St. John's Wood?

There were a few possibilities, one of which was a romantic connection to Burke. According to the maid we had questioned at the residence in St. John's Wood, Adele DeMille was an actress. Although a minor one.

Had she hoped to further her career through Burke? I shuddered at the thought.

Still, our inquiry cases had revealed that people, women in particular, desperate to change their circumstances, were often willing to do whatever it took. And that included relationships with men. Often with disastrous results.

Burke was well-known through the articles that he wrote for the Times. That might have been an attraction for someone hoping to change their situation.

The question was, what was her situation? Had Adele DeMille merely been using it until a better opportunity came her way?

What was her relationship with Burke? And why had it gotten him killed?

It was very near eight o'clock in the morning when Brodie suggested that we find a driver, as morning traffic had already begun to fill the Strand.

He was no worse, but no better for the pain. Yet, the bruise on his cheek had become quite colorful, with an added shade of green among the blue and purple.

Mr. Cavendish was able to wave down Mr. Jarvis, and we became his first fare of the day.

"Borough High Street, Southwark," Brodie told him as I stepped up into the coach.

Mr. Jarvis nodded as Brodie climbed in after me.

The bridge nearest the Strand was once called the Strand Bridge, according to Aunt Antonia and the stories she heard as a young girl.

It had been re-named Waterloo Bridge after the Battle at Waterloo and the military victory over Napoleon, although not without some controversy.

"Such foolishness," I remember her saying. *"Persons in a fit and falling in the middle of it because the new name commemorated a military battle. An important one, I might add, instead of naming it for a local landmark, as is the usual custom.*

"There are some who have nothing better to do than

complain about a name for a bridge, when there are far greater problems in the world."

Wisdom from someone who had lived through a great many things over the past eighty-six years, and now drove a motor carriage and took photographs with a camera. She was quite remarkable.

Brodie was familiar with Southwark from his early days with the MET, and we had been taken there as well in one of our inquiry cases.

As the city of London grew and had expanded, Southwark was a part of south London that was filled with docks along the waterfront, warehouses, taverns, and pubs. With tenements that gradually gave way to residences of a growing middle class, with the constant need for more housing.

Mr. Jarvis turned the coach onto Borough Road past a cross street that led to an old hospital, then past warehouses, a boatwright and storage, stables and a stable yard, then turned onto Borough High Street.

"This be the place, guv'ner?" Mr. Jarvis called down as he pulled the coach to a stop.

It was a familiar three-story galleried building with rooms for travelers at the second and third floors over the rooms of the tavern, when it had been a coaching inn with those railed walk-ways that looked out onto the gallery.

A wooden sign hung from the second story over the narrow, cobbled sidewalk below and was painted with the old image of St. George—the George Inn!

I looked over at Brodie and my earlier thoughts returned.

Had Burke brought Adele DeMille here? Again, for what reason? Was she here now?

We left the coach with instructions from Brodie for Mr.

Jarvis to remain, then walked the short distance to the entrance of the timber-framed inn under that sign.

It was exactly as I remembered, the smell of centuries of ale, with cigarette smoke and coffee, and quiet, as the usual customers had not yet arrived.

A handful of guests at the inn sat on bench seats in alcoves before a roaring fire on the hearth in the coffee room. Just beyond was the parlor, set with a table and chairs for suppers, that looked out into the gallery, just as Mr. Dickens had described it in one of his novels.

The barkeeper, a wiry man with shirt sleeves rolled back, and an apron, looked up from the scarred wooden bar where he had set out glasses and mugs.

"What can I do ye?"

In past cases, it was often necessary to create a story about the reason for our inquiries. Brodie could be quite resourceful in that.

We had discussed the possibility on the ride from the office, with the thought that we might encounter a tenement manager or building matron, as we had at Portman Square.

I gave the barman a smile.

"My husband and I are to meet my sister here," I explained and smiled again. We were informed that the manager at the desk just beyond the coffee room could assist us.

The manager had obviously left on some matter elsewhere in the inn. I rounded the desk and quickly found the guest book in the top drawer.

"As I've said before," Brodie commented, "ye would make a good thief."

"Well, certain circumstances call for certain measures," I replied. "According to a former thief I'm well acquainted with."

While Brodie made certain to watch for the return of the manager, I scanned the ledger for entries made in the guest book over the past several days.

I abruptly searched no further.

"What is it?"

"A. Burke, in room eight?" I looked up. "Is it possible?"

"Is there any other name that looks familiar, a woman's name perhaps?"

There was not.

At a sound from the hall, I tucked the guest book back into the desk and we left.

"The outside stairs to the second-floor landing," Brodie reminded me.

We had used those stairs during that previous inquiry case. We left by way of the door at the entrance to the coffee room, found the outside stairs and climbed to the second floor, where we encountered an older man and woman leaving their room.

Brodie smiled congenially, and we moved down the length of the hall to the door to room eight, waited until they had departed down those stairs, then knocked lightly. There was no response and I knocked again. There was still no response.

I looked over at Brodie. He nodded then tried the latch at the door. It was locked.

It took little effort to open, which I was certain would not have been comforting to other guests. Brodie called out. When there was no answer, he stepped inside the room. I followed and closed the door behind me.

It was simply furnished with a bed, table, and washstand, with clothes hooks on the wall beside the door for coats and umbrellas. The bed was neatly made as if waiting for the next guest, with a portrait of a country scene on the wall.

I gazed about the room, far from what Adele had known in

that manor house at St. John's Wood, a memory just there at the edge of my thoughts.

"It's the same."

Brodie looked at me as if I had taken leave of my senses.

"The name might be a coincidence."

He didn't believe it, nor did I.

"She's been here and quite recently."

It was the perfume that still clung to the air in the room.

"Perfume? Are ye certain?"

"It's the same scent I discovered in her bedchamber at St. John's Wood. It's very expensive," I then explained. "The sort of perfume a man might give a lover, and," I added with no small amount of sarcasm, "I would guess not usually found among travelers at the George Inn."

The question was, where was the woman who wore that perfume now?

We returned to the manager's desk. He had returned and looked up. I provided the same information we had given the bar man.

"Your sister, you say?"

He retrieved the guest book from the drawer, searched for that name A. Burke, then looked up.

"It's here, miss, room eight. Five days paid in advance."

This was the fifth day.

"I was told there was a laundry delivery made here," I inquired.

He nodded. "Two days ago. She left this mornin', said she would be back. But I've not seen her. Is there anything wrong, miss?"

"Did she say where she was goin'?" Brodie asked.

The manager shook his head. "She kept to herself while she was here, had meals sent up. Seemed in a hurry when she left, like she was afraid of somethin'. Been here thirty years. I know the look, seen it before."

"Do ye want to leave a message?" he inquired.

As if she was afraid of something? Or someone.

I had hoped we might learn something here, but it was not the first time Adele had disappeared. I was certain she would not return. But where would she go?

What had caused her to leave? Had something or someone frightened her? Had she heard rumors about the attack on Burke at the Old Bell?

I thanked him and we left the George.

It was well into the afternoon when we returned to the office. Mr. Cavendish met us on the sidewalk. There was a message for Brodie from Mr. Dooley.

He read the note. "He wants to meet at the Yard. It seems our 'old friend' has been making inquiries about the attack on Burke at the Old Bell."

That could only mean Abberline. This could add a complication to the investigation. Brodie frowned.

"I should meet with him. I can inform him of our visit this morning to the inn. There is no need for ye to go as well," he added. "I know yer feelin's about Abberline. Ye might be tempted to take a shot at the man."

Truer words had never been spoken. The man was *despicable*, that was the only word for it. In that first inquiry case, with my sister's life in danger, he had refused to investigate information we'd learned.

He considered her disappearance nothing more than a 'disagreement' between a husband and wife, common enough, as he had insultingly put it.

However, it was no common disagreement, and there was reason to believe her life *was* in danger, particularly after her maid's body was pulled from the river. Abberline had refused to investigate further.

And then there was his resentment of Brodie that had very nearly ruined him and sent him to prison, a convolution of lies fueled by old resentments.

Brodie knew me quite well. I might be tempted to take a shot at the man if I were to encounter him.

He motioned for Mr. Jarvis to wait. "There is someone else who may have information that could be useful."

There was no need for him to explain further, the vague words he chose conveyed a great deal.

"Mr. Brown?" I replied.

A man Brodie knew from the past, with a somewhat disreputable reputation, a name that was a disguise for his real name, which no one actually knew, with a reputation for business in all sorts of enterprises, mostly illegal. And someone we had previously done 'business' with when other efforts failed.

Or more specifically, I had *once* contacted and worked with. Brodie deliberately kept a distance between Mr. Brown and myself.

"Dealings with the man are not for ye," he had told me. "The less ye know, the better off ye are."

As for his dealings with Mr. Brown?

"We understand one another," Brodie had replied at the time. And no more was said, although from bits and pieces that I had learned of his past, I assumed what that meant.

Not a reassuring thought. And now he was planning on meeting with him once again. I did wonder about that 'understanding,' but did not ask. It was undoubtedly one of those things he did not want me to know about.

"Do be careful," I told him in parting. "I prefer you in one piece."

Bruises and broken ribs notwithstanding. There was that half smile at one corner of his mouth.

"Careful as church mice."

With Brodie, that was not necessarily reassuring.

After he left, I went up to the office. I had more notes to add to my notebook and on the chalkboard.

I organized everything we had learned on the board, with cross references to a second list that showed how the clues were related. And those clues we still had no information about.

It was well after six o'clock in the evening when Mr. Cavendish rang the service bell and reminded me that he was going to the Public House for supper. I asked him to bring a takeaway box when he returned.

The hound bounded up the stairs as Mr. Cavendish set off. Not that I was fooled. Food had been mentioned, and I was convinced he understood every word when it came to that.

"Very well, come in," I told him as I returned from the landing. He looked up at me with a self-satisfied expression. He was quite the con-artist, as Brodie called him.

He did have the uncanny ability to know exactly what was going on all the time. I was convinced that he understood everything that was said. We got along quite well.

Mr. Cavendish returned with supper, which I shared with the hound.

Brodie had not yet returned. It did seem as though it might be just Rupert and myself. Not that it was the first time.

"I'll be about if you need anything, miss," Mr. Cavendish assured me.

I had urged him to return to the Public House. He lived

there in a small flat with his new bride, Miss Effie. They were recently married.

He shook his head. "Orders from Mr. Brodie before he left," he informed me with a grin and the assurance that I was quite safe.

That was not the first time either. I knew well enough that he had a rather nasty knife tucked into the waist of his trousers. A *trinket,* he called it, acquired when he crewed on the merchantman ships that put in at foreign ports.

Trinket indeed. It had a curved blade several inches long with a handle of carved ivory. I had seen him cleaning it on more than one occasion. It was impressive.

"I've responsibilities now for the missus," he had said recently. "I'll not have her goin' about alone. One never knows what sort we might come upon."

I was reminded of that as I went out onto the landing, Rupert at my heel.

"A message was just sent round for you," Mr. Cavendish called up to me.

The courier services often worked late. However, I had no idea who would send a message at this time of night.

Was it something urgent?

I took the stairs, with a thought to Brodie and his opinion of the lift. There were times it was far more expedient to take them. Not that I would admit that, since the installation of the lift had been my idea. And it most certainly made it easier for Mr. Cavendish.

However, now...

He handed me the envelope. I quickly opened it and pulled out the note:

Please meet me—important.

Tonight. Drury Lane.

A.D.

I stared at those initials that seemed to shiver in the light from the streetlamp, along with that cryptic message.

Adele DeMille? Was it possible?

If so, who told her that I could be trusted?

There was only one person I could think of after what had recently taken place at the Old Bell—Burke and the bloodied note he had given me.

'What will you do now, Mikaela Forsythe?'

The note I now held in my hand had most definitely been written by a woman, the handwriting small, each curve of a letter flowing into the next, unlike that of a man, scribbled and almost indecipherable.

The pen had paused where the ink had puddled after that last word, as if the person who wrote perhaps had second thoughts before adding those initials.

And then there was that unmistakable scent of perfume, almost indiscernible, but I recognized it. The same that I had first discovered at the residence at St. John's Wood.

It was very near nine o'clock in the evening. There would be a play at the Theatre Royal, with guests arriving. The perfect place to meet someone in a crowd and not be seen?

"I will need a driver," I told Mr. Cavendish as I turned toward the stairs.

"Mr. Brodie would not want you takin' yerself off alone at night," he called after me as I reached the stairs.

"As soon as possible," I replied as I reached the landing at the office. I left a note for Brodie, then quickly gathered my bag and retrieved my coat from the stand. I locked the office door and returned to the sidewalk as Mr. Jarvis arrived.

"What should I tell Mr. Brodie?" Mr. Cavendish inquired. The expression on his face said far more.

"I've left a note." Not that he would be pleased.

There was another comment amidst much grumbling that I chose to ignore.

"You'll not leave without the hound," he announced. "Mr. Brodie would have what's left of me hide if I let you go off without him."

Rupert jumped into the coach, and I climbed in after. I gave Mr. Jarvis the destination of the Theatre Royal.

"That it is," he replied, and we set off, Mr. Cavendish still grumbling.

The theatre lights from the Royal lit up the night sky, as late guests continued to arrive amid the dozens of coaches and cabs on the street.

How was I to find Adele DeMille in the crowd? I thought as I stepped down.

I scanned those afoot around me as they rushed to the theatre entrance, along with those just arriving, and was very nearly run down by a late arrival. The coach pulled to an abrupt stop and the door opened.

"Get in, Lady Forsythe."

It seemed that I had just met Adele DeMille.

"Miss?" Mr. Jarvis inquired, with an eye to the traffic.

"It's quite all right. A friend," I told him as I stepped up into the coach with the hound behind me.

The driver efficiently guided the coach through departing rigs and then set off.

"A friend?" the woman across from me inquired with a faint French accent, her features concealed in shadows created by the light from streetlamps that spilled inside the coach window, then disappeared as the driver slowed the team.

"We are not enemies, Adele, therefore I prefer 'friend'."

There was a brief nod amid the cloak of darkness inside the coach.

"And you have brought a special friend with you?"

She obviously meant the hound.

"*C'est vrai.*" I replied in French, with the hope of putting her at ease. "*Voux avez demandé à se rencontrer.*" I reminded her that she was the one who asked to meet."

"He told me that you were educated. He did not mention that you spoke French."

I was not surprised, as Burke was most definitely not one to hand out compliments.

"The creature is yours?"

I heard the trepidation in her voice.

"A friend also," I replied. "He will not harm you."

A hesitant nod as Adele DeMille seemed to consider that, then called to the coachman to stop. At a glance I realized that we had reached the Strand, mostly empty now at this time of night.

"Perhaps if I had such a friend..." She seemed to gather herself. "I have heard rumors, and then when I did not hear from him..."

She spoke of Burke, no doubt.

"He's dead," I told her as gently as possible, without yet knowing what their relationship was.

"It is as I feared," she softly replied.

"Why did you leave the inn?"

She looked up and I caught the glimmer of something in her eyes.

Tears? I thought not. Burke was not the sort to cause that emotion.

Fear perhaps.

"You went there?"

"Lady's clothes were delivered there on a laundry order that I found on his desk. It seemed logical after the note he gave me when he asked to meet at the Old Bell."

"He said that you were very clever, and the only one who..."

"The only one?" I replied.

What did that mean, I wondered as I thought once more of his last words to me that night—*"What will you do now, Mikaela Forsythe?"*

There was obviously far more to this. And whatever it was, she was terrified.

"You asked to meet in that note you sent," I reminded her.

I wanted very much to know the reason, and what her part in this was.

"He said that I could trust you. And now...I am not proud of what I have done," she continued. "I did not know what would happen when it began."

I could only guess at part of it. That part Brodie and I had uncovered at the residence at St. John's Wood. Unfortunately, not uncommon. Even my friend Templeton had her relationships and affairs that she had proclaimed in a somewhat heated moment.

'I am not proud, but these things are necessary for some of us who are not born to wealth...' She had stopped and looked at me and apologized. She did realize that my own situation, in spite of what I had been born to, had been quite precarious, if not for Aunt Antonia.

And now? Someone not so unlike Templeton, who was obviously in danger.

Completely unexpected, she produced a thick brown envelope and thrust it at me.

"He said that if anything happened, I was to see that this reached you."

The sound of a coach approached. I heard the sharp breath she took as she cringed back into the seat of our coach, then slowly relaxed as it passed by.

"What is this?" I asked.

"Papers. There are drawings as well. I don't understand them, but I know they are important. They spoke of it many times."

They. Men she had entertained and now hoped to escape?

"Do not open it now. Perhaps Mr. Brodie will understand what they are. There is a letter as well, in German. I do not know what it says, but it is all very secret, and the reason they chose the house at St. John's Wood."

Where these people might come and go and not cause any suspicion? That seemed obvious.

I tucked the envelope into my bag.

"What will you do now?" I asked.

"I cannot return to the inn. There was a man who came and asked for me—he is German."

Was it Steiner?

I thought of the man who was seen at the Old Bell the night Burke was killed, and then again when Brodie was attacked.

"I had seen the man before," Adele continued. "At the house at St. John's Wood. I did not care for him. He was very...dangerous.

"The owner at the inn told him that I had left," she continued. One of the customers spoke of an attack at the pub.

"I had gone to purchase a newspaper, hoping to learn something, as I had not heard from Mr. Burke. When I learned that the one with the thick German accent had asked about me, I knew that I had to leave."

She had entertained these men, perhaps including Steiner, and in the process had learned something that terrified her. Something revealed in that thick package.

I reached across the aisle of the coach and squeezed her hand.

"You went to Mr. Burke."

She nodded. "He could be very difficult, but I knew his reputation. That he had exposed certain things."

Difficult didn't begin to describe him.

"He said that he had worked with you. That you knew people you could tell this to, and that if anything happened..."

He had arranged for her to stay at the George and had paid for it, another surprise.

Then, when she heard the rumors that he had been attacked, she was afraid that it was only a matter of time until the same people found her, and she left.

"Where will you go now?"

"There are rooms near the Adelphi where those in the plays stay. I will stay there until I can find a way to leave."

I was familiar with the apartments and flats near the Adelphi Theatre from a previous inquiry.

If Steiner had managed to find her at the George, it would be easy enough to find her in a flat near the theatre—a new face, the French accent, and then...

"You cannot go there," I replied, certain of it. "You will stay here for the night and then we will figure out what is to be done next."

"I cannot! They will find me! Steiner...!"

There was one thing I could assure her.

"You will be safe for the night," I repeated. "Mr. Brodie was once with the Metropolitan Police and has lived on the street. He will be returning soon, and he is the one person I would trust with my own life." And had, more than once.

"There is also the hound. His name is Rupert. He doesn't like strangers and can be quite fierce." He was also quite fond of sponge cake, but I did not go into that either.

"You will be far safer here than in a room near the theatre." Where her location would undoubtedly be revealed by anyone for a bit of small change.

At least there was someone here to protect her.

I was eventually able to persuade her, and we stepped down from the coach. I paid the driver and sent him on his way.

The traffic was thin on the Strand. The hound bounded across toward the alcove on the opposite side. I slipped that bound package into my bag and retrieved the revolver.

In the glow of light from a nearby streetlamp, I saw the surprise in the expression on Adele DeMille's face with the obvious question.

"I do know how to use it," I assured her and we crossed the Strand together.

As we reached the other side, I simply explained to Mr. Cavendish that Adele was a client.

"Has there been any word from Mr. Brodie?"

"Not as yet, miss," he replied with a curious glance at her. Yet he made no comment. Not that he wasn't quite used to various people we worked with arriving at the office.

"Please keep watch," I replied. "And do make it known if anyone arrives."

He glanced at the revolver that I held at my side and nodded his understanding.

"You might keep Rupert with you," I said in parting.

He had an uncanny instinct about people and would be the first to sound the alarm. With that, Adele and I climbed the stairs to the office on the second floor.

Once there, I locked and bolted the door and drew the shades down over the windows. I then took a chair from the side table where we met with clients and braced it under the handle.

I then laid the revolver on Brodie's desk. It sat across from the entrance, and if necessary, provided the best angle, as he had explained when I had suggested that we move it across from mine to accommodate other furnishings.

'It is best where it is, between myself and the other room, if there should be a need. And it provides a look through the window at anyone who might not be invited.'

I did see his point. It was that particular aspect of his inquiry business—it could be dangerous.

"You live here?" Adele asked as she glimpsed the adjacent bedchamber through the doorway.

"For now," I replied and did not go into details about the loss of the townhouse to fire in another case. That might have been unnerving under the circumstances.

I had her remove her coat and hat, then went to the coal stove. I added several pieces of coal, lit it, then returned to Brodie's desk.

The package lay there as well. It was tempting, but she had asked that I not open it. I respected her request. For now.

When coffee had bubbled and simmered sufficiently, I

poured two cups. It did smell quite bracing. I handed one to Adele.

She wrapped her hands around the cup and took a sip. "It is good, as I like it. And hot. I am very cold."

Adele DeMille was either a very convincing liar, or...

"Who are these people?" I inquired after some time had passed and I had filled both our cups once more.

She provided a physical description of three gentlemen who were the most frequent 'guests.' Hosts she described them, for their meetings. When others arrived, she was sent upstairs and not allowed to leave until everyone had gone.

The three who were there most often appeared to all be well educated. The others, one in particular, had a foreign accent. He was German.

And then there was Steiner.

"He was very cruel." She had set her cup down at the edge of the desk. "He came to my room. He wanted what the others took. He said that since he worked for them, it was a business arrangement."

There was no need for her to go into details. It was there in the anger and defiance in the expression at her face.

"And when he was through, he beat me. And then did this." She eased the neck at the bodice of her gown aside and revealed a gruesome scar of a wound barely healed.

It was the mark of a wolf's head! She'd been branded!

"He wears it on a ring on his hand," she added as tears slipped down her cheek. "It excites him to use it." She looked at me then.

"Is it a sin? What I have done with these men? And now Mr. Burke is dead." Her hands were clenched tight, folded before her.

How to answer that? There were so many things people did

to one another. Part of the harsh reality I had learned in the inquiry cases Brodie and I took. And now a question from a young woman, perhaps not so very different from myself.

Had I sinned when I had shot a woman in that first case? I thought not, considering what she had done.

I reached out and squeezed her hands.

"I think it is not a sin, when one is trying to survive. And you are not responsible for Burke's death. That belongs to another."

And Burke's own ambitions? Perhaps.

I rose and went to the safe Brodie had purchased and had brought to the office. For confidential papers that related to our inquiries, and money that he insisted we keep there, rather than at the bank.

Along with a handful of documents that included the title to the building, the signed registry certificate from when we married. And perhaps the thing that meant most to him—the plain bronze ring of his mother's that she always wore and had given to him before she died.

"It is most precious to me, this simple bit of paper," he said at the time, holding aloft the certificate. *"A memory that I will always carry. It is wot it means, and the words ye spoke with me."*

For a man who rarely showed any emotion or shared his thoughts, I was completely undone in the moment.

I had learned to handle myself with his stubbornness, that Scots temper, and his criticism over something that he was usually maddeningly correct about. But that moment...

I went to the safe, opened it, and retrieved the envelope with that gold button. I showed it to her, with that emblem identical to the mark on her shoulder.

"Where did you find this?"

"In your room at the house at St. John's Wood. I found it on the floor."

She slowly nodded as she held it.

"The one man lost it the last time…"

There was no need for her to say more—a man who had treated her as what he had paid for. A hostess for his friends, an actress to play a role and ask no questions, and of course…the rest of it.

"What are their names?" I asked.

How powerful were these men? And what were the meetings that were held there with them? And of course, the man known as Steiner.

She shook her head. "I never knew their real names. They called each other by other names—Sir Torch, Mr. Hammer, and Sir Saber. As if it were some child's game."

We were both startled by the sound of the bell at the landing. It ended abruptly followed by the sound of heavy steps on the stairs, and then someone at the door.

I reached for the small Webley revolver, held it with both hands, steady as I took aim at the door.

"Go into the other room," I told Adele. "Do it now!"

A key in the lock, a curse…and that thick Scots accent.

I pulled the chair back, and the door abruptly opened.

Brodie stared at the revolver in my hands.

"Bloody hell! Put the thing down before ye shoot someone."

That was the idea—however, not the irate Scot who stood in the doorway.

Mr. Conner grinned as he came up behind Brodie. "Always good to be prepared. Is that coffee I smell?"

Eight

"WOT IS the meaning of the names?" Brodie asked from across the desk in the office.

I sat in one of the wing-back chairs in front of the desk, while Adele sat in the other one beside it. Mr. Conner reclined on the settee, long legs stretched before him, arms folded across his chest, his head back amid loud snoring.

He and Brodie had returned a handful of hours earlier, both exhausted. Covered with stains of mud and other things from the streets on their trousers, and what looked very like coal smudged across Mr. Conner's face and beard.

To hide the glare of his white beard, he had explained with that familiar grin. Giddy as a schoolboy on an adventure. Brodie needed no coal with the dark bruise on his cheek and that dark beard.

There was no sleep, except for Mr. Conner, who had declared that he'd learned to sleep anywhere over the years. Brodie as well, the nature of having lived on the street. However, there was none since he now stared down at the contents of that brown envelope Adele DeMille had given me.

I had opened it earlier. It was her journal! Kept over the past year with entries, oftentimes no more than two or three words, but an account of what she had overheard at the house in St John's Wood.

It was in French, and it had been necessary for me to translate for Brodie as he leafed through the pages.

He stared down at it now with a frown as he sorted through what the journal revealed.

"The names you have here...what are their real names?"

Adele had been hesitant at first, speaking to me in French. Yet she knew who Brodie was from Burke, and I assured her that she could trust him.

She sat now in that wing-back chair, pale but resolute. Yes, that was the word for it—*resolute,* with the certainty that there was no going back after what she had already shared with me.

"Only one name I overheard, and it was by accident that infuriated him—Montfort. The one known as *Torch*. After that, I was not allowed to remain on the main floor whenever they met."

If she was correct in what she had overheard one of the other men mention, it might be Sir Richard Montfort, who was a member of Parliament, highly respected although considered quite a *firebrand*, a word that had been used to describe him. Ironically, in an article written by Burke.

He had also been appointed two years earlier by HRH Edward Albert, the Prince of Wales, to a committee that oversaw bills and expenditures for the military, according to another of Burke's scathing articles, as well as an advisory committee for the Royal Navy.

I did wonder about the name he'd taken for those he met with at St. John's Wood—Torch. A nickname to disguise his identity? But with a special meaning that connected back to that article Burke had written?

"What do you know about Gosport?" Brodie then asked, about that unusual location that she had overheard early in those meetings.

"I know only the name. Yet, it seemed important. They were very serious when they discussed it over several months."

"Ye have written 'B-10' in yer notes. Wot might that mean?"

"I found it written on a piece of paper that was thrown into the fire in the hearth. I don't know its meaning, only that it seemed important that no one else might find it."

I had set a pot of fresh coffee on the top of the stove. We had emptied the pot when he and Mr. Conner first arrived. This was the third pot over the past hours. No one had complained!

"And the last note ye made—18 April?" he then asked. "Wot might that mean?"

This month, I realized, and only three days away! What did it mean? What was the importance of 18 April?

"I only learned it in passing. I overheard them saying there would be no need for the house in St. John's Wood after that date."

"That is when ye decided to leave?"

She nodded as she stared down at her hands wrapped around the cup of coffee.

"The one who calls himself 'Torch' sent a man to my room, the one called Steiner.

She had told me about that harrowing experience and still wore the mark of it.

"He said that he knew I had been writing about things and demanded to see what it was. I hid it behind a loose panel in the wardrobe. My maid was the only one who knew. She must have told them.

"I lied and said that it was merely a letter to my brother in Paris. He did not believe me and tore the room apart searching for what you have in front of you."

Brodie had seen and experienced difficult things in his time as a constable, then inspector with the MET. Yet, even with that experience of things he refused to discuss with me, I knew he was affected by what she told him by the set of his mouth.

"I cannot go back there, Monsieur Brodie. They will kill me."

"No," he replied. "Ye cannot and will not." He looked over at me briefly. "We will see that ye are safe."

"But how?" she said with tear-filled eyes. Yet her expression was defiant. "You do not know them. You cannot understand what they will do if they find me!" As if to make certain he understood, she pushed aside the collar of the gown she wore over that dreadful mark.

"This is what they do—their butcher, the German. And worse. The one you call Steiner. He burned me."

I shook my head as Brodie looked over at me. Then I took Adele by the arm and spoke to her in French.

"Ça suffit pour l'instant."

That was enough for now. Then I persuaded her to follow me into the adjacent bedchamber.

She was exhausted, as we all were. Yet I knew that her exhaustion was different. It came from being horribly used, terrified, and then learning that Burke was dead. It seemed that she was already asleep before I pulled the blanket up over her.

Mr. Conner had wakened in the outer office as I returned from the adjacent bedchamber, and closed the door behind me so that Adele might get a few hours' sleep.

He was alert in the way that I had seen in Brodie, and I wondered if he had actually slept at all.

"What is to be done now?" I asked the obvious question as I returned to the chair that sat before Brodie's desk.

"The first thing is to make certain she is safe," Brodie replied and looked over at Mr. Conner.

"I could have her stay over at my flat," he suggested.

Brodie shook his head. "Ye've been seen about London, tonight particularly, and perhaps by the man, Steiner. It needs to be a place where even Steiner and the others would not only not think to find her, but would not dare to go."

"Mr. Dooley might be able to have her protected until we can learn more wot this is about," Mr. Conner replied.

"With wot the coachman told ye about where he delivered Steiner, best to stay low for a while. The fewer know about this the better, my friend," Brodie told him.

"In other words, I'm out of a job."

Brodie smiled. "Wot ye dinna know canna hurt ye, aye?" The smile disappeared then.

"I am grateful for wot ye learned about Steiner, but I will not put ye at risk. The woman's notes prove out wot ye learned. But we dinna know how this one who calls himself '*Torch*' is involved."

"I could tell ye that it is my choice to make," Mr. Conner replied.

"Aye, ye could. But yer thirty-odd years older."

That grin again. "Aye, but I've the experience of those thirty-odd years, and...I dinna fight fair."

There was a look that passed between them.

"All right, but I will help find the woman a safe place. Wot do ye have in mind?"

"There is a man we both know..."

In that language of men where little is said, but much is understood, Mr. Conner seemed to know exactly what he was thinking.

"Aye, yer right in that. There's no one would risk going up against the man and his fellow cutthroats."

I was certain who they spoke of—a man who was known to control criminal activities across London and who had never been caught. Mr. Brown.

Brodie was thoughtful. "She will need other clothes." He looked over at me.

I had clothes—trousers, shirt, and jacket borrowed from Brodie that I had worn in the past.

Mr. Conner glanced toward the door to the bedroom. "When do ye want me to take her?"

"As soon as possible," Brodie added.

"Ye'll need to let the man know," Mr. Conner commented.

Brodie nodded. "Mr. Cavendish will know how to get word to him."

It was mid-morning when I wakened Adele and explained what had been decided.

"Who is this man?" she had asked of Brown.

That did require an explanation before she was comfortable.

"I have heard stories about such a man in Marseilles, where I am from. It is said that those who threaten him are not seen again."

That did seem to describe Mr. Brown, whom I first met through Munro. He and Brodie had an odd friendship that came from 'past business,' as Brodie called it.

Mr. Brown conducted business in rooms over a tavern he

appeared to own in the East End, with an assortment of *foot-soldiers,* as he referred to his men, and 'business' interests that included shipping and various other enterprises. Among them were rumors of bootleg liquor brought in from France, along with other illegal cargos.

When I had asked Brodie about some of those enterprises, he had simply replied, "Tis best ye dinna know."

I was aware that he had done 'business' with Mr. Brown in the past in a somewhat odd partnership—favors passed back and forth, with that reminder from Brodie—"Dinna ask."

Brodie had sent Mr. Cavendish out with the message for Mr. Brown. He returned just after midday.

"The docks at St. Katherine's. His man Spivey will meet Mr. Conner there."

"And he understands that she is not to be bothered in any way?"

"As ye told me, and he's agreed. Along with the reminder that you now owe him a favor."

I was concerned what that might require, but I did not ask as I provided Adele with the clothes for her 'disguise'—Brodie's cast-off clothes that I had altered so that they would fit and not fall about my ankles. Adele and I were about the same size.

"You are married to him?" she had asked. "A lady and a former police inspector?"

"Yes," I replied. And I had been on that adventure ever since.

I had explained that first inquiry case that involved my sister without most of the details, only that he was the only person who helped me find her. I did leave out that other part that was quite personal.

"I should like to find that sort of man," she had replied.

I had assured her that she would be safe with Mr. Brown and that we would see each other again when this was over.

As for her journal—those hasty notes, including the names of those who were responsible for Burke's murder—it was presently locked in our safe at the office.

Adele wore no makeup, as she had when I first met her. Gone as well was the gown from one of London's most exclusive shops. I had given her a pair of my boots, and with the jacket, acquired from a seconds shop, the somewhat battered cap with her hair tucked under, she might have been any 'lad' on the street, selling newspapers for the Times, or pinching food from a vendor. I added a smudge of coal dust.

"A new role for me to play," she said as she glanced in the mirror on the dressing table.

I thought of the characters in Mr. Dickens's books, taken from his travels about London. She could have played the part of any one of those poor street urchins he had written about.

"I assure you no one will recognize you, and you will be safe enough with Mr. Conner."

It was late in the afternoon, darkness lowering over the building across the Strand and along the street when Mr. Conner finally returned.

"The package was safely delivered," he informed us.

I let out a sigh of relief. He had been gone for some time, and I had begun to worry that they might have encountered some difficulty with Steiner still out there somewhere.

"No difficulty," he assured us with a familiar grin. "Brown does have some of the finest ale to be found."

Of course.

Nine

─∾─

15 APRIL, THREE DAYS UNTIL...

WHAT WAS to happen on 18 April?

And what was important about Portsmouth? More particularly Gosport, which was very nearby?

Some sort of shipment, possibly illegal contraband?

That hardly seemed likely, as it was in the heart of the Royal Naval shipyards. It would surely take some level of insanity for someone to attempt that right under the noses of the Royal Navy.

"What is important about Portsmouth?" I asked over breakfast that Mr. Cavendish had brought for us in a carton from the Public House.

I'd had a restless night after Mr. Conner departed the previous evening with Adele DeMille to escort her to Mr. Brown's pub, where she would be safe. Her smile in parting had struggled as she thanked me.

"You will always be my very good friend."

Mr. Conner had returned hours later, to assure us that they had arrived without incident. Adele was provided a room above the pub, where he informed us he had remained for a while and had sampled the finest whisky. A surprise, he announced, that Mr. Brown would have a drink of such high quality!

I had looked at Brodie after Mr. Conner left for his own flat to get some sleep.

"Very fine whisky?"

"It might have been something that Munro arranged?" he had replied.

And now?

I had not added notes to the board regarding what we had learned more recently, nor about my encounter with Adele and her subsequent, most recent 'disappearance.'

While the office was far more secure than most places, and with Mr. Cavendish's presence on the street below, there had still been occasions when others found their way in.

With Steiner still out there somewhere, along with what we had learned from Adele, Brodie suggested that we keep what we now knew to ourselves, with nothing written down that others might want to know.

"The question now is, what is at Portsmouth that is worth killing for?" he said from where he sat at his desk, chin propped on his hand, dark brows drawn together as he looked at me.

We often had the same thoughts.

Waterloo Rail Station was the nearest that connected direct to Portsmouth.

I had quickly dressed, and we left the office, Mr. Jarvis delivering us across the river in time for the next departure.

It was a journey of between two and three hours, far more expedient than a packet or steamer to the Solent, and then a transfer for a brief rail trip, or coach to Portsmouth, and then Gosport nearby.

Before departing the office on the Strand, I had placed a telephone call to my great aunt—my daily call for any word from Lily.

There was none, but she had informed me that she had taken more photographs with her new folding camera, and was it possible that Mr. Brimley might be able to process the film?

In that conversation I had also inquired whom she was acquainted with in the Royal Navy who might be at Portsmouth.

"Your new case, dear? Portsmouth? That might possibly be Admiral Reginald Ormsby..." She had then corrected herself. "Possibly not. He's been dead for over twenty years. The time does seem to fly past." She had given the matter further thought.

"Sir Thomas Mountbatten might be able to assist, if he's not off to India."

Yes, well...I thanked her.

"You must give my camera a go," she said in parting. "It could be useful when you and Brodie are off on one of your adventures."

The call had ended there, the earpiece on her end obviously left dangling as it clattered on the table where it had been installed after much persuasion. And then a familiar voice, Mrs. Ryan, previously my housekeeper at the townhouse.

"Is everything all right?" I inquired, concerned that Aunt Antonia might have taken a tumble.

"Quite all right, miss. She's taken herself off into the gardens with her camera, and then we are off to Miss Lenore's so that she can take a photograph of Miss Charlotte." She had then added, "Is there word about a new residence for yourself and Mr. Brodie?"

I assured her that we were investigating different possibilities and hoped to make a decision quite soon. A slight exaggeration.

"Excellent!" she announced. "I have found that your adventures are quite mild in comparison to those of her ladyship."

She had then informed me, "She has made it known that she wants Mr. Hastings to accompany her about London for the next photographs she wants. She insists that he learn to drive the motor carriage."

I had the deepest sympathy for Mr. Hastings, my great aunt's head coachman, who, it appeared, was being catapulted into the new century by way of a motor carriage.

"Is there a difficulty?" Brodie inquired as the call had ended.

"None at all, unless one considers Aunt Antonia unleashed on the streets of London in the Benz motor carriage."

I could have sworn he smiled. "Something I have to look forward to as well for yerself?"

I ignored that comment as we had set off across the river.

Waterloo station was crowded with morning travelers departing for various parts of London and beyond, Portsmouth merely one of those destinations.

We made our way through more than a dozen booking offices with numbers above for the destination. Those on holiday, others in business suits, and others gathered in lines to purchase tickets. A series of overhead boards contained arrival and departure information.

Brodie constantly scanned the faces of those around us, his hand tight about my arm, as he guided us through and we found the ticket office for Portsmouth.

He requested a compartment rather than the usual coach fare.

It was a bit costly, but I did not question his choice. I had learned there was always another thought behind everything he did.

We quickly found the boarding platform for our train. It had arrived earlier. We found our compartment. Brodie pulled the inside shades down, then took the seat across from me. He laid his revolver on the seat beside him, under his right hand.

There was a knock at the door a few minutes later as the train prepared to get underway. He took no chances that we might have been followed, or that someone involved with all of this might have boarded the train as well.

His hand closed over the revolver. He angled it behind him just out of sight to whoever was in the passageway, then slid the door open, glanced past the attendant, then handed him our tickets.

Two hours or more until we reached Portsmouth. In that way that he could sleep anywhere, Brodie returned to the bench seat across, stretched his legs before him across the aisle, the revolver once more beside him, and appeared to fall asleep. So much for conversation.

"Do ye miss taking yerself off on yer adventures?"

Some time had passed since leaving London, and I was surprised not only that he apparently had not been dozing, but by the question. I might have laughed, except that he seemed quite serious.

"I have thought about taking myself off to Australia," I replied. "If it didn't take quite so long to reach it."

"Wild creatures as well as wild men?" he commented from under the brim of the hat he wore, that dark gaze just above the yellow and purple mark watching me.

"What could possibly compare to animals such as Burke or Mr. Brown?" I replied. Linnie's former husband, or our father. The lowest of the low.

There were others, of course, over the past handful of years since I had first inquired about his inquiry services. The list was quite long.

Never one to miss a detail, "And wot of wild men?" inquired the man whom some would consider part of that same club, one of those who had lived outside the mold of what was considered a gentleman. With fine clothes, a proper education, a title, and polished manners that often hid secrets.

I would take a gentle man with fire in his eyes, education that came from the streets, and manners...well, there was that part, but with arms that held me until I thought my bones might break but didn't. Then, his way rushed with an intensity of something more that lay just beneath the surface, almost as if he was afraid that I might disappear. And that dark gaze that made it impossible to look away, or want to.

I shared the thought that came with it.

"*You* are my adventure."

And for a moment, it did occur to me that if there were a few more hours to our journey, it would be necessary for him to set the latch on the compartment door.

"Ye are a bold one, Mikaela Forsythe."

It was barely an hour later when I felt the train slow, and the attendant announced at the passageway that we had arrived at Portsmouth. Then that faint jarring motion, and we stood to depart. Brodie paused at the entrance, as he had before, then turned.

He brushed my cheek with the back of his fingers, a gentle touch from a gentle man.

Portsmouth was quite large, spread along the coastal shore of the South Atlantic and the Solent, that large channel that linked to the Isle of Wight, where the Queen was known to stay, and east with Gosport just beyond.

The streets and roadways were filled with the usual traffic found in a busy seaport city, including those who lived there, trams, wagons laden with barrels, shopkeepers, vendors, along with crews from private merchant ships.

As well as sailors from a half-dozen ships of the line moored at the docks, taking on supplies for destinations, possibly to some of the places I had visited. Their wooden hulls gleamed in the afternoon sun, while riggers made repairs to sails.

The attendant at the station directed us to a line of cabmen and drivers for passengers who disembarked. Brodie found a coachman who made a regular run to Gosport.

"Not many such as yourself or the lady go there," he added. "Only them who work there."

Brodie thanked him, and we climbed aboard.

The entire southeastern point from Portsmouth, past the Solent and beyond, was a maze of piers, docks with moored Royal Naval vessels, dry docks with ships under construction, warehouses, and manufacturing buildings with smoke pouring from giant stacks.

We passed carters and wagon drivers, along with short-haul rail lines that carried larger cargoes, as well as vans and wagons with work crews. It was a city unto itself, extending along the coastline, with signage made up of letters and numbers, a sort of street code, that directed drivers and haulers to different areas. And included three large structures that loomed over bays that had been sealed off from the harbor.

"Dry docks," Brodie commented. "What was that number that Adele wrote in her journal?"

"Gosport, B10," I replied.

He signaled to the driver.

"Not allowed beyond, sir. This is a restricted area by order of the Royal Navy."

"We need to learn what B-10 refers to," Brodie said beyond the hearing of the driver.

"It could tell us wot the men who met at St. John's Wood were about."

The question was how to go about it, in an area that was restricted.

I did have a thought on that, not brilliant, and certainly not one that I would usually undertake.

Yet, if we were to learn what importance that number meant, we needed to be creative. It certainly wasn't the first time, as I thought of that name Aunt Antonia had mentioned.

"Tell the driver that I am the daughter of Admiral Ormsby, and we're to meet him at B-10."

"Who the devil is...?"

I smiled. "Trust me."

After all, what was the worst that could happen? That our driver would refuse?

I listened as Brodie gave him the information. He returned and quickly climbed into the coach.

"And wot if Admiral Ormsby learns of it?" he demanded as the coach set off toward that last covered dock.

"That would be quite remarkable," I replied. "The man is dead."

"Bloody hell..."

There was more, muttered in Gaelic. The coach rolled to a stop, and we stepped down.

The roadway was just as congested here with wagons and vans, workers departing and arriving, along with shipments of various pieces of machinery. The signage before one of those enormous, raised tents indicated that we had arrived at B-10.

Berth 10, I thought from my travels that had included sea travel. It was obviously a construction site by the activity that we saw, but *what precisely*? I thought.

What was important about B-10 that three men had been secretive about when they met at St. John's Wood, and had ended in murder?

Brodie had asked the driver to remain, as I waited for an opportunity to enter that enormous structure. Obviously, a woman, perhaps other than the Queen, would be an unusual sight in such a place.

I stepped into the shadows behind one of those enormous sliding doors at the entrance. The opportunity arrived as a half-dozen workers emerged, talking amongst themselves as they left.

Brodie glanced my way as I gathered my skirts in one hand and quickly slipped inside, then suddenly stopped at the sight before me.

The dry dock was much like the others we had passed, except for the vessel that lay within it.

It was almost the full length of the dock, sleek, made of what appeared to be steel, fully enclosed with a tower that rose from mid-deck—far different from the masted, wood-hulled ships of the Royal Navy that we had seen upon arriving at Portsmouth.

As ridiculous as it seemed, it reminded me of a metal cigar tube, not unlike something I had read about...

"It's a submarine!" I exclaimed. Brodie had followed me inside.

"Wot is a submarine?"

"It's meant to navigate underwater. I've read about it, but had no idea that it actually existed." Or almost, as it was obviously under construction.

A sign at the dock nearest was painted HMS-B10.

It was beautiful and at the same time terrifying, and far different than any ship of the line, or any other, for that matter, at Portsmouth.

We had discovered B-10. But what did it mean?

"We obviously were not meant to see this, but it could be important to our inquiries," Bordie said in a low voice beside me.

"We should leave now."

"Right, you are," a deep voiced startled me. "Now, slowly turn around with your hands raised."

It did seem as if the *admiral* I had boasted of had found us. Or, at the very least, a half-dozen uniformed men with firearms aimed at us.

Ten

THERE IS an old Chinese proverb I had learned in my travels, that the best defense was a good offense.

I thought of that now as I sat across from Brodie in an anteroom outside the office of Sir Avery at the Tower of London. Where we had been delivered under armed supervision after being discovered in what was obviously a secret, secured area at Gosport.

We had been detained, telephone calls had been exchanged, along with the intervention of Sir Laughton, the family attorney, and someone else whose name was not mentioned, but who I strongly suspected might be the Prince of Wales.

We were then transported back to the rail station at Portsmouth and escorted onto the next train returning to London, where a police van waited to bring us to an emergency meeting with the director of Special Services.

The door to his office, deep within the ancient and imposing walls of the Tower—ironically built by my ancestor some eight hundred years before—was suddenly wrenched open. Sir Laughton appeared, features drawn due to the late hour of the night.

I did wonder what our offense was to be as we both stood.

"I have presented the facts as you gave them to me regarding your presence at Gosport. You should know that his Royal Highness has spoken on your behalf, due to special circumstances."

"Are we to know wot those circumstances might be?" Brodie inquired with his usual calm.

"It will be explained to you both. My suggestion is to be straightforward. Answer the questions, tell the man what you know. Not speculation." His next comment was for me, with a weary smile.

"However, my advice would be 'the less said the better,' on behalf of your present client."

He then added, "I have spoken with her ladyship in spite of the late hour," Sir Laughton shook his head. "I must say, she was not surprised, and I am reminded of some of her early 'adventures,' which I assure you are the cause of all my white hair." He bid us farewell.

"I will speak with the both of you afterward as regards Mademoiselle DeMille."

Alex Sinclair, a Special Services agent, appeared at the doorway.

We knew Alex from previous cases. He was young, quite brilliant, and had invented an incredible code machine for the Service. It was all quite clandestine.

The Service had been created in the aftermath of several dangerous incidents in Europe and answered only to the Queen, or with increasing frequency to the Prince of Wales, who had been at the center of that first inquiry case with Brodie.

There were other incidents where a case we pursued had crossed paths with that of his Royal Highness and the Special Services Agency. And now?

It did seem as if we might have *stepped in it,* as my great aunt frequently commented. That, of course, was a reference to her association with horses since childhood and at Ascot, where her horses regularly appeared.

I was more than familiar with that from my own childhood and the stables my father kept, as well as the usual refuse one had to be careful of in the streets of London.

It was an appropriate description of the present situation. The question was, what had Brodie and I stepped into?

"Straightforward answers," Brodie reminded me in a quiet voice as he slipped a hand under my arm, and we entered Sir Avery's office. Alex closed the door after having obviously been disinvited to this part of the inquiry.

Sir Avery was not at his desk as in the past in this sort of meeting, but instead stood before one of the few windows that looked out onto the green and that scaffolding where several notable persons had been hanged for a variety of crimes or possibly on some royal whim in the past.

He was as tall as Brodie, thin under his worsted suit of clothes, hand thrust into the pockets of his trousers in the way I had seen before in others when they either didn't know what to do with their hands, or perhaps to prevent strangling someone.

Sir Avery was a precise, decisive man with gaunt features behind a full beard that had once been the color of his dark hair but was now streaked with white. I did wonder if Brodie and I might be the cause of that. It was an interesting thought.

When I would have spoken, Brodie shook his head—the wisdom of a former police inspector.

He had once explained that silence was often an advantage. Wait out the other person, since there was a great deal to be learned from their first statement. Therefore, we waited.

"I have the authority to have both of you brought up on charges of trespass and interfering in highly secret activities."

That dark gaze met mine. *'Wait'* it said, and we continued to wait.

"There are those who have faced a firing squad for what you have done."

He slowly shook his head.

"But for the grace of the Almighty, and the intervention of his Royal Highness, I can do neither, due to your connections to the Prince of Wales."

I was certainly relieved to hear that.

He continued to stare out that window with that steely gaze.

"I will hear your explanation of the situation now." He slowly turned about, that sharp gaze fixed on Brodie.

"What the devil were you doing in Portsmouth? Trespassing into a secure area at the naval yard where no one is allowed other than workers." His voice rose with each statement.

"And then entering a site that is off-limits to everyone except essential personnel!"

Then before either one of us could respond, that sharp gaze fastened on me.

"Lady Forsythe. It does seem as if you refuse to keep to your inquiries about missing jewels and hysterical wives whose husbands have strayed."

Brodie's fingers closed sharply around my wrist. I could almost hear his warning not to let my temper get the better of me at Sir Avery's belittling comments.

"It is our understanding that Sir Laughton has presented the facts to you," he calmly replied. "They are as he explained them."

"I would hear them from you, Mr. Brodie!" Anger exploded, but Sir Avery was not finished.

"This agency is specifically tasked with protecting the interests of the Crown, interests which at times must remain secret to accomplish what must be done. You have interfered in that!"

I angled a look at the expression on Brodie's face in an effort to determine just how precisely he would respond to that direct attack by a man he admittedly did not trust.

His expression was completely void of all emotion, that dark gaze direct and unwavering as he stared back at Sir Avery. Then, respectfully but succinctly, he replied.

"I would remind ye that Lady Forsythe assisted in exposing a plot against the Royals and, in due course, was severely injured during an assassination attempt against His Royal Highness. And with all due respect, if the Agency was doin' their job, as ye say, there would have been no need for our present inquiries...sir!"

I fought not to burst out laughing. He had, in a very direct, succinct manner replied as Sir Laughton had recommended. Although perhaps not precisely as Sir Laughton intended.

That first inquiry case that involved my sister's disappearance had been difficult...very near almost deadly.

I had been injured with a bullet wound to the shoulder, my first direct encounter with Mr. Brimley and his remarkable skill. The wound had healed quickly with no lingering impairment.

Not one to carry on about such things, I chose to ignore what had happened. However, Brodie had not forgotten, nor forgiven himself for not being there at that precise moment and taking the bullet himself.

Even now, a handful of years after, in private moments, he lightly touched that scar, and there was something in his expression. *"I might have lost ye."*

As for the present situation, I wasn't at all certain that Sir Avery would survive the moment, a vein standing out on his forehead.

He eventually managed to bring himself under a measure of control as he looked down at what appeared to be a report with the Royal Navy seal at the top. He then sat down at his desk, hands steepled before him, that sharp gaze fastened on Brodie.

"I must insist that you explain the present circumstances of your inquiry case."

Straightforward, Sir Laughton had cautioned. Only as much as necessary.

Brodie gave me a reassuring nod and indicated one of the chairs across from Sir Avery.

I knew precisely what he was about, subtly sending a message to the man. I sat and then Brodie continued.

"Lady Forsythe received a request to meet with Mr. Theodolphus Burke of the Times newspaper. Upon her arrival, it was discovered that Mr. Burke had been attacked and severely injured."

He continued to explain the note I received that contained the name of a woman. How, in the interest of learning who the murderer was, we had proceeded to the woman's residence, where we discovered that there had been a disturbance and she had departed.

The remainder of the details were sparingly revealed and

included the name of a witness to the murder and the discovery of his identity.

"Maximillian Steiner," Sir Avery repeated, not surprised. "A man known to us." And then continued.

"I am informed that news of Burke's death has been withheld."

"It was reasonable to assume that those responsible might be drawn out if they thought he was still alive," Brodie responded.

"A plausible assumption perhaps." He turned to me then. A bit of divide and conquer?

"What of your visit to Gosport, Lady Forsythe? And disregarding that it was a restricted area? A highly serious offense?"

The sarcasm was obvious as he pressed for more information. I did wonder how much Brodie would tell him, including the contact Adele had made with me the night before.

I was quite thorough with this interrogation, yet determined not to reveal more than absolutely necessary for Adele's sake.

"The combination of the letter and numbers was discovered along with information for the date of 18 April," I explained.

"And with your vast experience in world travel, you were able to conclude that it was necessary to go to Portsmouth," Sir Avery snapped.

"I read somewhere that naval vessels are usually known by a series of letters and numbers before they are named and christened by the Queen."

It was a bit of a stretch of the truth, actually more than just a bit. However, I left it at that. Let him think whatever he would.

"As for the facility at Gosport, there was no restriction, and no one was about to inform us that we were not allowed to enter." True as far as it went.

"So, I am to believe that you put together these vague clues and assumptions, then took yourselves to Portsmouth to determine what else might be learned in the matter of Mr. Burke's death?"

Brodie said nothing. I smiled.

"Do you take me for a fool? Am I to believe that the both of you possess such superior intelligence that you are able to discern something from scattered bits of information?"

I was tempted to respond to that, but did not.

"Mr. Brodie, Lady Forsythe, you are the beneficiaries of certain persons in very high places."

I exchanged a glance with Brodie as Sir Avery threw down his ink pen in obvious frustration. Then picked up the flared end of a speaking tube on his desk, attached to a long copper line that connected through the wall to some distant point.

"Alex Sinclair," a voice responded, garbled yet recognizable.

"Send in Admiral Williams." Sir Avery tossed down the tube as I looked over at Brodie.

There as a faint sound from the hallway outside, and the door abruptly opened. The gentleman who had escorted us from Portsmouth, along with a sufficiently armed guard, entered the office.

"Please be seated, Admiral," our host greeted him, then stood and rounded the desk. He shook his head as if deeply aggrieved.

"I have received specific instructions from His Royal Highness that all pending charges against Mr. Brodie and Lady Mikaela Forsythe are to be dismissed. They are further to be provided every accommodation in the pursuit of their inquiry into the death of Theodolphus Burke. Along with full cooperation by this agency until the matter is resolved."

When the admiral would have objected, Sir Avery shook his head.

"Sir, I have my instructions. You, of course, may refuse to cooperate, in which case I suggest that you take your objections through proper channels and to HRH the Prince of Wales."

"You have my full cooperation," Admiral Williams replied, his expression quite taut.

"Now, Mr. Brodie," Sir Avery turned to him. "How may we assist you in this?"

I caught the change in the expression on Brodie's face, the frown that appeared. The slight against myself was not lost on him, that less than subtle omission that both of us were involved in this new case.

"Lady Forsythe has made an observation from our visit to Portsmouth that would seem to be important."

"What would that be?" Sir Avery replied.

"She might be able to better explain."

"By all means, Lady Forsythe," Admiral Williams stiffly replied, obviously less than keen to indulge a woman. Not the first time I had encountered that, and undoubtedly not the last. However...

I retrieved the notebook from my bag and opened to a blank page. I then took out my pen and began to draw as I explained.

"I was quite young when I first saw the illustration in a book by Jules Verne in Lady Antonia Montgomery's library. It was written in French, and it took me some time to get through it. But most fascinating." I added more details to the drawing as I remembered it.

"The illustrations were by an artist, Alphonse de Neuville,

and absolutely fascinating. You may be familiar with it?" I looked up and caught the change of expression on the admiral's face.

"Even though the book was published over twenty years ago, the author did have a spirit for adventure and a fascinating imagination." I added a finishing touch, then passed my notebook to Admiral Williams.

"It would seem, sir, that the Royal Navy is in the process of building a submarine."

He stared down at my admittedly somewhat crude illustration, drawn from memory because of my fascination with the book. He eventually looked up and handed the notebook to Sir Avery.

"You are very observant, Lady Forsythe," he eventually commented. He did not deny what Brodie and I had seen. There was another look exchanged with Sir Avery, who nodded as I retrieved my notebook and tucked it into my bag.

"The project was begun two years ago after much discussion with the Prince of Wales and others, in response to growing challenges to our colonies in the Far East and the Mediterranean."

He appeared to measure what more he would tell us.

"With certain innovations and developments in steam-driven engines, it had become quite clear that the days of Her Majesty's sailing ships were limited. In addition, recent confrontations supported that, and it was determined that the Royal Navy needed to pursue advancements in our ability to address those confrontations.

"It was an undertaking of the Prince of Wales, with Her Majesty's approval, to begin a transition to the new technologies, and specifically included the development of an underwater vessel with the ability to navigate areas unseen. B-10 is being built for that purpose."

"Ye made the comment that our inquiry case has intersected with that of the Agency," Brodie reminded Sir Avery.

"The goal for the construction of B-10 was to keep the project secret. There are those in other places who would be very keen to know about the project," Sir Avery explained.

"You are familiar with Mr. Sinclair's work," he pointed out. "He has learned that there has been conversation in foreign places with information about B-10."

"Every precaution has been taken to make certain that no information has been divulged," Admiral William added. "Those working on B-10 have been thoroughly scrutinized."

"Yet, you had knowledge of B-10 through your investigation into Mr. Burke's murder."

"Do ye have yer suspicions regarding the person who may be responsible for that information being known?" Brodie inquired.

Another look passed between the admiral and Sir Avery.

"There is someone who has been part of the planning and development of B-10 from the beginning. This person would have specific knowledge and access to all aspects of the project." Sir Avery hesitated, then continued.

"This person is integral to the development of B-10 and highly regarded."

He hesitated once again. "He is also a cousin to Her Majesty. It is highly unlikely, but must be considered, that the information he has may have been compromised. It is to that end that we have been making our own inquiries. I am certain that you understand the delicate nature of the situation."

A most delicate situation indeed.

"If we are to provide assistance, I must ask that ye provide us with all information that ye have."

"You do understand the serious nature of this, Mr. Brodie? You have stumbled into something that could have serious ramifications."

"It would seem that it is past the time for that concern," Brodie then told him, "I will expect the information first thing in the morning. If ye decide against it, then we will continue with our own inquiries."

"You are leaving?"

Brodie's hand closed around my arm.

"Unless we are being further detained. In that case I will ask for Sir Laughton to return."

"That won't be necessary. I will see that you have all the information that we have. I will send Mr. Sinclair."

We encountered Alex Sinclair in the hallway as we left.

"I apologize. I was not aware what Sir Avery was about. If I had known, I would have tried to warn you, even though there are things I could not tell you about."

I did appreciate it, even though it would have been impossible to warn us after we left for Portsmouth.

"We will be working together," Brodie shared with him. "We will see you in the morning."

A coach and driver were provided for us. We sat together as we departed for the ride to the Strand.

In spite of his bruises and broken ribs, Brodie pulled me against his side and wrapped his arm around my shoulders.

"You were quite magnificent," I told him as we set off.

It was well after midnight, and I was exhausted from the day's 'adventures.' There was nothing quite like being surrounded by several armed men of the Royal Navy, shackled, then taken aboard a return train to London, and all but accused of conspiracy, and whatever else Sir Avery might have considered.

"Do you trust him?" I asked as I rested my head on his shoulder.

I was fairly certain I already knew the answer from past experience with the man. There were only a few Brodie trusted, hard lessons learned in the past.

"I trust the word of His Highness," he replied. "Sir Avery will not go against him." His hand was warm as he took mine.

"And I trust ye. Although I must admit that fer a moment there when the Admiral spoke to ye as he did, I thought it was a good thing that he was sitting in the chair. If he'd been standing, ye might have dropped him to the floor with one of yer moves."

"I did take that into consideration," I replied.

"I thought as much. But then when ye explained yer observations and wot ye had read in a book, he knew that he'd been taken down a peg."

"I was not trying to take him down a peg...well, I had perhaps considered it. He was quite pompous and full of himself."

"And offended yer womanly intellect."

He was right of course. It did seem that the ladies had a long way to go before our ideas, opinions, and experiences would be accepted on the same level as a man's. We just needed to help that along whenever we could.

"And now?" Brodie inquired.

"It is not my womanly intellect that is offended, it's my appetite. I'm starving."

There was only a marginal comment from Brodie as we returned to the Strand and then promptly entered the Public House across from the office.

The fare of the evening was stewed chicken with vegetables and dumplings.

Brodie started to make a comment about that fourth dumpling, but I gave him a warning look.

The problem with stewed chicken and dumplings was that I could hardly keep my eyes open as we returned to the office.

Mr. Cavendish greeted us, and Brodie informed him that Alex Sinclair would be meeting with us in the morning.

He then joined me in the lift and escorted me into the office.

I reminded him that there were notes I needed to make.

"In the morning, lass," he said as he laid my clothes aside, then his own as well and joined me.

Next to Brodie, chicken and dumplings were really quite marvelous. Not that he would have appreciated the comparison.

Eleven

THURSDAY 16 APRIL, TWO DAYS UNTIL…

ALEX SINCLAIR ARRIVED PROMPTLY the next morning. He had matured since we first met, no doubt in part due to his responsibilities at the Agency, with a neatly trimmed moustache and a few lines about the eyes he had acquired along the way.

Still, that shock of dark hair had a habit of falling across his forehead, as now, when he entered the office and went directly to the side table where he deposited a portfolio of papers on the edge of Brodie's desk.

"The information is to be kept secure at all times, and no one else is to know. Sir Avery was very specific about that. And I am to make certain that everything is in order when I return with it."

He smiled, and I was reminded that at one time I had thought he might make a good match for Lily. However, I was reminded then, and now, that she had a mind of her own regarding such things.

Our last conversation in regard— *"I have no need for a man. They are overbearing, thick-headed, and refuse to listen to anything I say. I've gotten along well enough without and will continue to do so."*

I thought of Brodie with that somewhat accurate description. Yet, there were other things she might eventually appreciate. Though she had assured me there were none.

"I have taken care of meself since I was seven years, and I can take care of meself now."

That had been when she first arrived in London several years past. Though in the time since, with her education and some refinement, it seemed her opinion had not changed.

Now, as I greeted Alex, I did realize that he might have had his hands full with her, even though he was highly intelligent, very pleasing to look at, brilliant with his inventions, and quite adventuresome considering his work for the Agency. In particular, the coding machine he had invented and now connected to our electric.

"And I'm to assist in whatever way that I can," he added. "I've been making inquiries regarding the...matter at hand. That is if you are agreeable to sharing information you have learned."

A suggestion. I suspected it had not been a 'suggestion' from Sir Avery, but rather an order.

Brodie nodded. "Start with the chalkboard and the notes ye see there. There is other information as well that we have chosen not to disclose there."

"Of course," Alex replied. "I understand after working with you previously." He then went to the board and read through the notes I'd made.

"And admittedly, the matter is most serious. Still," he grinned, "I would like very much to see a submarine. Even better, take a voyage in one!"

Over the next two hours, Brodie explained what we had

learned, beginning with that note Burke had sent with the urgent request to meet, only to find him mortally wounded when I arrived. And then the bloodied note with Adele DeMille's name.

Alex nodded. "The man does have quite a following, and now to have disappeared? There are rumors all over London."

"*Had* an extensive readership," Brodie clarified, and then explained Burke's death that night.

"Oh, I say," Alex exclaimed, obviously surprised. "Sir Avery said nothing about that."

"I doubt he knows of it," Brodie replied. "The body is presently in the morgue at the Yard under another name, along with the body of Jardine."

"Oh my, Sir Avery will not be pleased to learn that, with the Yard very nearby," he commented then looked over at me.

"You say that Burke gave you a note that night?"

Brodie showed him that bloodied note.

"St. John's Wood?" he commented.

I explained what we had found there, followed by our inquiries about that gold button. Our brief meeting with Jardine at Savile Row, his sudden disappearance, and then his body pulled from the river that same night.

"He obviously recognized it," he frowned. "He then fled and encountered someone who didn't want you to know what his part in this was, along with those he knew."

Brodie had opened the safe and retrieved the button with that unique image embossed in the gold. He handed it to Alex.

He frowned. "We've seen this before."

Brodie and I exchanged a look.

"Where?" I asked.

"A good part of my work at the Agency is disseminating information..."

He hesitated, no doubt instructed to reveal as little as possible.

"What sort of information?" Brodie asked, not to be put off over something that could be important.

"Sir Avery insists on 'need to know.'"

"Two people are dead, the danger is still out there, I would say that is a need to know," Brodie curtly replied.

"Yes, of course. You are quite right," Alex admitted, then explained.

"We receive regular dispatches from the Continent from our people in other places, which I'm not at liberty to say. The wolf's head is a very old symbol, particularly as shown here, quite crude actually…"

"What does it mean?" I demanded.

"In some cultures, it represents strength and power," he continued. "It has been found on ancient war shields, the hilts of daggers, and that sort of thing. More recently, there have been similar symbols found in communications that were intercepted."

"Which cultures?" Brodie then asked.

It did seem this was something more Alex was not to divulge. And then decision made.

"There is a particular group that operates in the shadows—underground, if you will. The first indication of their existence was discovered literally by accident in Hamburg. A roadway accident that involved a person one of our people was following over another incident.

"The man in the accident was carrying certain papers, and that image was found on one particular piece that seemed to indicate that *things were in place, but far more information was needed.*"

"Did it say wot those things were?" Brodie inquired.

"Only that it would be helpful once all was known, and that there were those who would finally be brought down. That was over a year ago. It was considered important enough that we've had our people search for more information. That gold button is the first connection we've seen."

"What about the man in the accident?"

"Unfortunately, he died in hospital, and we were not able to learn anything more."

"Or perhaps it was made certain that he died," Brodie suggested.

Alex nodded. "It would seem possible, with what you have discovered."

Brodie explained that Mr. Conner had then found the coachman who had driven the man we now knew as Steiner from the Old Bell the night Burke was attacked. And that we had made inquiries with Herr Schmidt at the German Gymnasium, who knew the man.

Alex nodded, obviously having recognized that name.

"Steiner is a name we have followed, though we have no idea what he looks like. We had not heard that he was here."

I explained that Steiner had attacked the man who remembered seeing him the night Burke was killed, a man called Fitch. And that Brodie was injured after he intervened and attempted to stop him.

"Fortunate that it was not worse."

While there was more to that, there was no point in going into further detail.

I then explained about the laundry ticket that led us to the George Inn, where Adele DeMille had been staying after fleeing from St. John's Wood."

Alex stared at me. "A laundry ticket? Who would have

thought? And you say that she then came to you? The woman from St. John's Wood?"

"Burke had given her my name."

He looked from me to Brodie. "Was she able to tell you anything about what Burke was up to? A story for the newspaper, perhaps, that he was after?"

Brodie and I exchanged a look.

Adele had entrusted us with her life. I was not willing to break that trust.

However, the journal had contained that date of 18 April, that was only three days away, as well as the names of the three men known as Torch, Hammer, and Saber, obviously not their real names, along with that combination of letter and numbers, B-10, that we now knew the meaning of.

The questions now were: who were they, and what had that secret project to do with all of this?

"The work you've accomplished is incredible," Alex told us. "Where is the woman now? Sir Avery will undoubtedly want to speak with her."

"She is safe," I replied, but refused to tell him more. Not that I didn't trust Alex, but neither Brodie nor I fully trusted Sir Avery, whose loyalties lay with the Crown no matter the cost in lives.

"There are three names she was able to give us." I was willing to give him that, as it was obviously critical to what was to take place 18 April.

"Three men who met at St. John's Wood over the past year, though there may be others. The names were obviously meant to disguise their identities. She said they called one another Torch, Hammer, and Saber."

"Torch?" Alex stared at him, obviously stunned. "You're certain of that?"

Brodie nodded. "Do ye know it?"

Alex nodded. "Twelve days ago, I decoded a cross-channel communication from one of our people in Brussels. We've been following communications that surface from time to time, for information that could be in the interests of the Crown."

"You're spying," I commented.

Alex looked at me, somewhat startled from behind his glasses.

"I suppose that is what some might call it. In any event, we exchange information that could be useful to those we trust over there as well."

"Tell us what you know," I insisted. "Not Sir Avery's approved version," I added. "All of it."

He squirmed ever so slightly and reminded me of the young man we first met, fresh from university and quite wide-eyed over the prospect of working for the Agency.

"The word 'torch' is one we picked up several months ago, but with nothing to go on, no way of knowing that it was in fact the name someone went by until we decoded this recent message, and it specifically referred to the fact that 'Torch' would make certain everything was handled.

"There was no mention of Hammer. This is the first I've heard of it. But obviously from what you've been able to learn, it would seem to have something to do with the one known as Torch."

But who was Torch? And what was important about those secret meetings at St. John's Wood?

"What about Saber?" I asked of that third name Adele had revealed.

Again, Alex shook his head. "There has been no mention in anything the Agency has received."

"B-10 is obviously a secret project." Or at least it was supposed to be, except for our discovery of it, for which we had been temporarily taken into custody by Naval authorities.

"What is the purpose of B-10?" Brodie inquired.

"I cannot..." Alex began, then stopped. "I do see your point. When finished, it will support a crew underwater with the ability to move about unseen."

"Jules Verne," I commented. His imagination soon to become reality.

"Who else would have an interest in it?" Brodie pressed him.

It was obvious this part of the conversation was not what had been intended as far as Sir Avery was concerned.

"It could be of interest to other governments or agencies."

A man who disguised himself with the name 'Torch,' a naval vessel with the ability to enter any port without being detected.

Spying indeed, I thought, and it had become deadly.

Brodie was thoughtful.

"It could be beneficial for another government to have B-10."

"Steal it?" Alex remarked with more than a little surprise. "That would be impossible. The Solent and all of the naval yards are heavily guarded. No one is allowed..." he hesitated. "With the exception of yourselves, of course. An accident that will not be repeated. In any event, B-10 is not yet seaworthy, and there will need to be tests run."

"Wot about those involved with the development of the thing?" Brodie asked.

"Everyone associated with B-10 has impeccable records, from the designers to the High Lord of the Admiralty, and Vice Admiral Lindhurst, who has experienced some illness."

"You've met Sir Williams. He's been part of the project from the beginning, and liaison to the Home Secretary as well as HRH the Prince of Wales."

"What sort of illness?" I inquired regarding Admiral Lindhurst.

"A severe case of gout, unfortunately, that has not subsided. The poor man cannot walk, and it was decided that his position should be overseen by Vice Admiral Williams."

Was it possible that there was something to this? A convenient illness, and then being replaced by another man?

An impeccable record with the Royal Navy. It seemed that everyone with connections to B-10 was investigated, and had passed scrutiny.

"Does the date 18 April mean anything to you?" I explained.

"We've not received any reference to that in any communication." Alex looked from me to Brodie. "What do you know about it?" he asked.

That was the problem; we didn't know anything about it. Only that it was an entry in Adele's journal.

He would undoubtedly ask to see it. There was even the possibility that it could be used against her because of what it contained. I was not willing to risk that.

She had been caught up in a situation not of her own making, and her life endangered. If certain things were made known, her life might be in even greater danger because of it. Still, she had come to me in spite of the risk.

18 April was obviously not the date for the launch of B-10.

What else then could be so important about that date that it had been spoken of in secret? Who were those men who had met secretly? And what was the secret that was worth killing over?

"Sir Avery will be quite surprised at what you've managed to uncover," Alex said then as he closed his file. "And naturally you will provide any additional information that you learn."

"Naturally," I replied, aware that we had in fact learned far more about the situation than the Agency. If Alex had provided all the information they had.

I was inclined to think not. It was not a criticism of Alex. He was merely doing as he'd been instructed. It was from experience.

"Perhaps not," Brodie commented after Alex left. "We need to learn more about Steiner."

It was near midday when Mr. Conner returned to the office. It did appear as if he'd had little sleep, and almost certain when he shared that he'd remained at Mr. Brown's establishment for the previous night.

"Adele?" I inquired.

"Well and good, under the protection of himself."

Which obviously referred to Mr. Brown.

"I'll not ask about the favor ye did the man, and now himself in return," he told Brodie then waited.

"Bah!" he exclaimed when Brodie did not respond.

"And ye'll not share a word. It must be a considerable favor ye granted the man. Though he was forthcoming about something that could be important."

"Wot?" Brodie asked.

"About the man, Steiner. He may be secretive about certain things, but less so when it comes to others."

"Wot might that be?"

"It seems that the man has a certain preference for things in women." He hesitated and looked over at me. "It might be best to discuss it between the two of us," he told Brodie. "Man to man."

Oh, for heaven's sake, I thought.

It wasn't as if I hadn't heard of certain things. It did come up from time to time with our inquiry cases. Still, Mr. Conner refused to explain. I caught the bemused expression on Brodie's face.

"How did Mr. Brown come by the information?" he asked Mr. Conner.

"It seems that Steiner encountered one of Brown's 'ladies' and struck an arrangement. Then, afterward, even though the 'accommodation' was apparently most satisfactory, Steiner refused to pay."

That, of course, did not explain what the 'accommodation' entailed.

"And the woman is one of Brown's favorites, a real high earner. She's been with him for some time, and he swears that she's trustworthy."

I bit back a comment.

A business transaction, a buyer and seller—the oldest profession known to man.

"You might want to speak with her yerself," Mr. Conner added with a cautious look in my direction. "Could be there's more she could tell us. She has a flat near Covent Garden."

Twelve

COVENT GARDEN, I thought, as Brodie and Mr. Conner departed.

There had been a somewhat sheepish look from Mr. Conner as he suggested that a visit to the woman who worked for Mr. Brown could be useful. For Brodie's part, there had been obvious amusement.

Not that I wasn't fully aware that he was a man of some experience...there was that woman in a chartreuse gown I had encountered when I first inquired about his investigative services.

Or rather, I should say that she was more 'out' of that chartreuse gown than in it, spilling over in several places.

I was no prude. Still...

"Ye have that look," he had commented as Mr. Conner waited at the sidewalk below and Mr. Cavendish secured a driver for their 'visit' to Covent Garden.

"What look is that?" I inquired.

"The look that says if ye still had the revolver ye might be tempted to use it. A good thing Alex returned just the one revolver."

"I have no idea what you are referring to. Any information you might be able to acquire regarding Steiner would be helpful, other than his '*preferences*' about certain things."

Brodie was amused by it all.

"There could be something to be learned," he said with mock seriousness. "And then shared."

"And pigs fly," I replied.

He laughed and paid dearly for it as he winced at the pain it caused in his ribs.

"It serves you right," I told him.

He completely ignored that and his ribs as he pulled me against him.

"Someone I know insists that pigs do fly."

He kissed me then in a way that it was undoubtedly best Mr. Conner waited on the sidewalk below.

And when it ended, far too quickly, he looked at me for several moments in that way that made my toes curl.

"Bloody damn, Scot," I whispered.

That smile...*wicked* might be the word for it.

I made good use of the time after they left, adding what we'd learned from Alex to my notebook, searching for something more in the information that might provide another clue that could be useful.

Based upon Alex's information, we now knew that inquiries had been made about 'Torch' from a contact in Brussels.

The message had been extremely vague and provided no other information, except that it had been sent by someone who assumed the information was secure.

That raised questions in itself. What could possibly be so important?

A natural assumption was that it was something the man known as Torch was working on, obviously important enough to remain secret with the use of that alias.

Another assumption was that it might possibly be someone of high importance. If his true identity was known, it could possibly have serious ramifications.

And then there was the entry in Adele's journal about B-10, which we now knew was the newest generation of the Royal Navy—a submarine.

By Alex's own admission, once it put to sea, it would enable the crew to maneuver undetected under the surface of the ocean. The possibilities that would offer seemed endless.

Who were the men at St. John's Wood who spoke of it? What had Burke intended when Adele went to him? Had he intended to write about it? Or was there another reason he asked me to meet him at the Old Bell that night?

'What will you do now, Mikaela Forsythe?'

The ringing of the bell on the landing jarred me from my thoughts. And then there was someone at the door barely visible through the glass covered with the usual grime from coal fires and spring rain. Accompanied by Rupert who barked incessantly.

It was not the sort of bark when a stranger approached. The hound obviously knew the person, who wore a bright purple jacket with a purple hat over hair tucked under that had once been dark auburn but was now streaked with white.

That striking blue gaze looked back at me through the glass in the door somewhat myopically, through thick-rimmed goggles that gave my great aunt the appearance of a large bug. An elegantly dressed one, but a bug nonetheless.

"Good afternoon, dear," she greeted me, stretching up on the toes of her boots to kiss my cheek.

"The lift is quite marvelous, no need to climb all those stairs. Mr. Cavendish was good enough to accompany me, so there was no mishap. And Rupert as well."

She sailed past and proceeded to unwind the netting that draped her hat and protected that magnificent silver-and-red hair.

"Lady Spencer has spoken of a salon that grooms dogs! I can acquire the name for you. Dear Rupert could use a bath."

Dear Rupert had entered the office with her and now sat at her feet, tail thumping on the floor. He was quite fond of her and had spent considerable time in the past at Sussex Square, particularly during the recent recovery from an injury.

He looked up at her with soulful dark eyes, and she indulged him with a *petit four* cake. In addition to my housekeeper's sponge cake and biscuits I indulged him with, it was a wonder he was not as big as a horse.

Aunt Antonia had also removed her goggles and placed them beside her hat on Brodie's desk. She had obviously driven her motor carriage from Sussex Square. There were mud splatters on her right cheek. I provided a handkerchief.

"Thank you, dear. I did leave without one."

Which, of course, begged the question, what was she doing here?

"A last-minute alteration. The gown simply would not do, and Madame had worked on it for weeks."

Two questions, I realized, that required some information.

"Yes, of course," she replied. "I ordered the gown months ago with the final fitting just the week past, but it needed to be taken in once I tried it on, you see. I picked it up from Madame, just this morning."

Not exactly.

I adored my great aunt. She had taken my sister and me in after the deaths of both our parents. She had provided us with an education, travel that first whetted my appetite for adventures, and had sponsored Linnie when she came out a few years before—a dreadful mistake on my sister's part, as her husband turned out to be not only unfaithful, but might have gotten her killed as well.

Antonia Montgomery, now eighty-seven years old, had never wed or had a family of her own. We became her family.

There were those who thought her quite eccentric, driving about in her motor carriage, experimenting now with her folding camera, or indulging herself with Old Lodge Whisky, a very successful and lucrative enterprise when she should have been sipping port.

And of course, there were her plans for her final send-off, whenever that might occur, by way of a Viking longboat she'd had built specifically for the purpose—off in a blaze of glory.

"And now, with the event at St. James's Palace very near... You do have your gown?"

I had to admit that I had neither a gown, after the fire at the townhouse had taken everything, nor an invitation. I was presently reduced to wearing clothes that were at the office at the time, with a few purchases made since. Nor was I aware of the 'event,' since I had not received an invitation.

"Oh, dear. Your invitation was sent with mine from the Lord Chamberlain, after word of the fire at the townhouse.

"What event?"

"The reception for the German legation at St. James's Palace, in two days. It will be quite an affair, with members of the Royal family in attendance, with their connection to the German royal family.

"Lenore and James will be attending," Aunt Antonia continued. "She informed me that her whole existence seems to be nappies and preventing catastrophes with Charlotte fully mobile—the child does remind me of you. And then, of course, with the next one on the way. She needs to get out and about one more time before the babe's arrival.

"She has already complained that she feels as large as an elephant. It is a pity that most of your clothes were lost in the fire," she continued. "You can hardly attend in the clothes you are wearing now."

I momentarily recovered from my shock at the news that a reception was to be held the following evening at St. James's Palace. Was it possible that was what the date 18 April meant? Was something to happen during the reception?

And what was it Aunt Antonia was saying about the clothes I was wearing?

"You can hardly wear a walking skirt and shirtwaist to the reception. It is formal attire, dear. With your sister's present condition, Madame created a very flattering, elegant gown for her.

"Most certainly Lenore would be thrilled for you to wear one of her other gowns. You are about the same size. I will contact her as soon as I return to Sussex Square. Of course, there is the question of what Brodie will wear. Don't worry," she went on. "I shall mention it to James. He will undoubtedly be able to come up with something. This is so exciting!"

She leaned in and kissed my cheek. "I must be off and deliver my gown into Mrs. Ryan's very capable hands for a final touch with the smoothing iron before tomorrow evening."

A reception the following evening...18 April!

~

BRODIE

"There is a woman who has worked for him in the past, according to Mr. Brown," Mr. Conner explained. "She chose to leave his 'employment' after some disagreement over missing payments.

"He heard through one of his other 'ladies' that she was no longer working the streets but had gone exclusive with one particular customer, a German fella," Mr. Conner added.

They had arrived in St. Giles, a poor working-class part of London. They stepped down from the hired hack. According to Mr. Conner, the woman they were looking for lived in a one-room flat in a tenement off Whitecross Street.

"Brown's 'employee' saw him once when she encountered them on the street near Covent Garden. It seems there was a nasty argument, then they went off together."

"The woman's name?" Brodie asked, not that it would be her real name. Women often used aliases, either to hide what they did from their family, or as advertisement.

Imma Good was one name he recalled from his days with the MET—clever and sad. *Miss Plenty* was another. Both had ended badly, one lost to drugs, the other from the diseases that were often part of the profession.

"Kitty is her name," Mr. Conner replied. "This is the place." He indicated a rundown tenement. "Another tenant I found also recalled seeing Steiner about. First floor, one of the 'finer' flats according to the woman I spoke with, where Kitty moved just a few weeks ago at the insistence of her 'gentleman' friend."

As Brodie knew only too well, the word *'finer'* could mean many things in comparison.

The tenement reminded him of countless others, jammed

side by side in the poorer parts of London, so that it seemed they held the next one up, and if one collapsed, all on the same street would come down as well. He had once lived in a place very like the one they entered now, as Mr. Conner led the way to that first-floor flat.

This is the one," he said. "The woman should be here this time of the day. Perhaps Steiner as well," he cautioned, removing the service revolver that he'd retired with from under his coat.

Brodie retrieved his revolver as well, so generously returned by Sir Avery.

"I'll keep the watch out here," Conner whispered, from experience in the old days with the MET.

Brodie knocked on the door, then stood to the side of the threshold. He'd once seen a fellow constable shot through a closed door. The man had survived, but it was a hard lesson learned...one of many.

There was no answer. He then tried the latch. The door opened slightly. He exchanged a look with Mr. Conner, then pushed the door open further.

The all too familiar smell struck them first, the sort of stench that reached to the back of the throat and had nothing to do with usual squalid conditions or stale food.

Kitty's naked body was sprawled on the floor, and by the smell and the look of her, she had been dead for several days. Left where she fell, she stared with blank eyes, blood dried on the floor from the cut on her throat.

"It would seem that Steiner has left the building for the last time," Mr. Conner commented in that detached manner of one for whom the scene was all too familiar.

He searched the rest of the single room as Brodie crouched down beside the body. There was something clutched in the woman's hand. It was a piece of cloth perhaps torn from Steiner's shirt as they struggled?

The cloth was fine, the sort a man who was paid well might wear. And there was something more. Something cut into the woman's skin?

"Nothing," Conner announced. "The man is thorough when it comes to covering his trail." He paused and gestured to the body.

"What is that mark on the woman's breast?"

There was no electric in the flat. Conner took out the hand-held he carried on his nightly travels among London's finest pubs. Some habits were hard to break.

He held the light over the upper body as Brodie gently probed the mark with the tip of the blade of his knife. It was not a cut.

"It appears to be the image of an animal," Though the mark was slightly distorted from the discoloration and deterioration of the body, he recognized it. He had first seen it on that gold button Mikaela found at St. John's Wood.

It was the image of a wolf's head, and it had been burned into the woman's skin.

Thirteen

IT WAS WELL into the evening when Brodie returned.

I had supper brought from the Public House across the Strand after Aunt Antonia departed, and put the portion remaining in the cold box she had insisted be installed when she gave ownership of the building to Brodie.

Brodie was quiet and moved about stiffly, in the way I had seen the past two days since his encounter with Steiner outside the Old Bell.

He had removed his coat and cap.

It was doubtful he'd eaten anything after leaving with Mr. Conner earlier.

"Mr. Cavendish was good enough to bring supper back earlier. There's a plate in the cold box."

When I turned to go into the adjacent room, he caught me by the hand and pulled me against him in spite of my reminder of his broken ribs. He said nothing, then lowered his face into the curve of my neck.

His hair and beard were damp even though it had not rained recently, and he smelled of soap—the same scent of shaving soap that I had noticed Mr. Conner used even though he had a moustache.

With a full beard, Brodie rarely used shaving soap, or the Sunlight Soap for bathing in the shower compartment, as he refused to smell like the lavender soap that I used.

Although he had been known to break that rule when he had joined me in the shower compartment. That had been some time in the past, as that particular pleasure had ended with the fire at the townhouse.

He continued to tightly hold me, and I was concerned it might cause him further injury.

"What is it?" I inquired. "Has something happened?"

I had been concerned when he went off with Mr. Conner after learning where Steiner might be found.

"Mr. Conner?" I then asked. He was not a young man, and if there had been an encounter...

Brodie's hold gentled, though he kept one arm about my waist. He brushed my cheek with his other hand.

"Do ye know how fine ye are to me?"

There was something in his expression, something dark and...wounded. That was the only word that came to me.

I knew the answer to that, improbable as it would have been before that first inquiry case a handful of years earlier.

I brushed his beard with my fingers in that way that had become a language of its own between us.

"Your hair and beard are wet," I said as my fingers moved along the curve of his jaw.

"Mr. Conner allowed me to wash at his flat. I couldn't come back to ye smellin' the way I did after wot we found... I won't let it touch ye."

It seemed that my worst fears had come to pass, although not in the way I first thought.

"Steiner?"

"Gone, by a few days before we arrived."

"And the woman he was with?" Although I was certain what the answer would be.

"Dead. Probably the last time he was with her."

There was more, but for now it could wait.

"I'll warm supper for you and pour a bit of Old Lodge." But when I would have moved away, he pulled me against him once more and held onto me.

He had not touched the supper I placed before him on his desk. Instead, he poured another dram of whisky for both of us.

He eventually told me the rest of what they found at that crumbling tenement where a woman named Kitty had entertained Steiner exclusively. And the mark left on her body. He had then closed his eyes, his head on the chair back.

"I may have learned something about what is to happen tomorrow—Saturday evening, 18 April."

That dark gaze opened, narrow, barely a slit that fastened on me as I continued to explain the visit from my great aunt.

"I didn't know about it, as the invitation would usually have been sent to the townhouse. Instead, it was included with her invitation sent to Sussex Square."

There was no 'aha' moment, no other exclamation. He simply listened.

"It makes sense," I then added my thoughts. "We know that three men of position were meeting in secret at St. John's Wood. From Adele's notes, we know that it has something to do with the submarine the Royal Navy is having secretly built at Portsmouth. Along with the three men who went by the aliases of Torch, Hammer, and Saber."

Secretly did seem a moot point after our trip there.

"And according to Alex, the Agency has received coded messages about a man who goes by the name of Torch."

And that date, also disclosed in the things Adele had over-heard and then put down in her journal before she sought out Burke.

Had she sinned, as she had tearfully asked? And then caused Burke's death?

I could never accept that and would defend that what she had done in the end took more courage than many of those I knew.

I had added notes about what Brodie and Mr. Conner had discovered at that flat in St. Giles, including the description of that mark that had been burned into Kitty's body. I then added my own thought about that.

I do believe there is a special place in Hell for those like Steiner. As Lily had once said about the death of a friend from an early experience in Edinburgh before she came to London.

People like Steiner, those who procured his services for their own purpose, and anyone who would commit murder and leave a young girl terrified in the shadows had no soul...only the evil that fed them.

Quite profound from one so young.

As I finished my notes, I looked up. The fire was low in the coal stove and the room had taken on a sudden coldness.

Brodie had still not touched the supper in front him, the glass tumbler empty, his handsome features drawn.

Aunt Antonia had telephoned earlier to say that she had spoken with my sister. Linnie was thrilled with the news that we would be attending the reception at St. James's Palace.

She had no way of knowing the reason, of course. That we hoped to discover the importance of the date to those three men at St. John's Wood.

She had promised to send a gown over in the morning that I might wear, and surely there was something her husband had that Brodie could wear, with such short notice and no time to purchase a formal suit of clothes from a tailor's.

I closed my notebook. I went to the stove and closed the two doors across the front to hold in the heat, then set the lock on the door. I left the plate of food where it was. Rupert would appreciate it in the morning.

Brodie eventually stood. He had not spoken after he first returned, but had simply listened as I explained what I had learned from Aunt Antonia, and my thoughts on what that date meant. I reached for his hand.

Other than the barest details of what he and Mr. Conner found, he had kept the rest of it locked inside, determined, as he was so often, to protect me from the more gruesome part of it.

"Do you know how fine you are to me?" I told him and laid my hand against his cheek.

"There are things we need to talk about," Brodie insisted.

I knew perfectly well what he meant, and where it came from.

But not tonight, I thought, as I led him into the bed chamber and unbuttoned his shirt.

Then held him against me as he had held me so many times.

It was his habit to rise early, often times having not slept at all, a holdover from his time with the MET and other things.

This morning was no different, as I awakened to find him already dressed in trousers and a jumper, his hair quite wild about his head.

He had placed a call to Alex Sinclair earlier.

"I'm to meet with Sir Avery at the Agency when I arrive. He needs to know wot we've learned."

"You could remain here and let him dangle over what we now know."

"And wait to see what yer brother-in-law has found for me to wear tonight?"

I had shared that part of Aunt Antonia's plan with him.

"The man is a bit shorter."

"I thought instead that we might simply lock the door, lower the shades, and…"

"Och, ye are a brazen lass."

"What I would have suggested is *sleep*. You tossed about most of the night, after…"

He returned to where I sat on the edge of the bed, the blanket held against me, and leaned toward me.

"After?" A dark brow lifted in that maddening way.

"You know very well what I mean."

"If ye are feeling neglected, Lady Forsythe, I suppose that I could be persuaded to accommodate."

The smile was there, the way it lifted his mouth at one corner. Yet different, with that cut below his eye.

"In your present condition, I might injure you further," I replied in consideration of those broken ribs.

He laughed and then winced. "Aye, for a moment last night there was the possibility that ye might have done me in."

With that, he left, just out of range of the pillow I hurled at his head, which landed on the floor beside the doorway.

I attempted once more to dissuade him from that meeting, but he would hear none of it.

"There could be something important about the reception tonight. We have no way of knowing all those involved. And I gave me word to the man in exchange for the information he provided us."

"He has no loyalty to anyone, except to Queen and country. I doubt he had any feelings for his mother."

"I know yer feelings toward the man. Mine are much the same. But dinna look at me that way."

"What way is that?" I replied, quite out of sorts over the matter.

"As if ye'd prefer to dump the man on the floor or run him through."

I tried not to laugh. He was right, of course.

"He uses us and then is just as likely to hang us out to dry," I objected, determined to make my point. "It is about power, and he uses it for his own end."

"Aye, a government man to be certain. But I have the advantage that I know it and use it against him to protect meself and you."

"Oh, very well," I conceded.

"Will ye be waitin' in bed for me?"

"That offer, Mr. Brodie, has come and gone. At any rate, Linnie is sending clothes over this morning for us to wear tonight."

And he was gone.

I knew my sister's taste in clothes quite well. She preferred soft, pale colors with lace and ribbons attached, while I preferred more subtle colors, devoid of lace and ribbons. My lack of appropriate clothes might not have been necessary except for the fire that had taken everything at the townhouse.

"You really must make an appointment to visit Madame," Linnie had added at the end of that telephone conversation. "She knows your measurements and could easily provide you with gowns and other clothes, instead of the clothes you kept at the Strand before the fire. And you should pay more attention to those things, Mikaela. What must Mr. Brodie think that you have little to nothing to wear?"

I knew precisely what Mr. Brodie thought of that, but did not say it. After all, she was well into her second pregnancy and had lamented about being quite uncomfortable.

Although the prospect of the evening reception at St. James's Palace seemed to have lifted her spirits.

The clothes were sent to the office by way of her housekeeper, who had never been to the office on the Strand. She arrived by way of the lift after Mr. Cavendish announced her arrival, the garments well wrapped in cloth against any stains or dirt and carried over in her arms.

She was a tall, stout woman I had previously met when calling on my sister. A Godsend, Linnie had announced, who managed their household, allowing both Linnie and James to spend time with their small but growing family, as well as the demands of James's publishing company.

Through Mrs. Evers they had also acquired a nanny who was a perfect match for young Charlotte's energy and precocious nature.

"Mrs. Warren has included ladies' delicate wear as well," Mrs. Evers announced. "And sent a note." She handed me an envelope, then slowly approached the chalkboard.

"Oh, my. How very exciting. She did explain that you are presently on a new inquiry case with Mr. Brodie?"

Her comment was obviously an attempt at further information which I did not share.

"How do you do it?" she then inquired.

Carefully, I thought, but didn't say it.

"Most of the experience is with my husband. He was once with the Metropolitan Police."

"Oh, yes. Of course. Mrs. Warren did mention that."

And to avoid further questions, I took the garments from her, then laid them across the side chair in the adjoining room. I closed the door behind me as I returned to the outer office, the bed still somewhat rumpled. In fact, quite rumpled.

"Thank you so very much, Mrs. Evers."

"Yes, of course," she replied. "And I must be on my way as well."

When she had gone, I read Linnie's note. The gown she had sent for me had been ordered when she was first pregnant with Charlotte.

'I grew enormously with her and was never able to wear it. And admittedly it is not my color, although Aunt Antonia was quite adamant at the time. James insists that I must have had a momentary lapse when I had Madame make it for me. Therefore, you now have a new gown.

'I am so looking forward to this evening. It will undoubtedly be my last public appearance until after the baby arrives.'

Oh, dear. I had no way of knowing what to expect if Aunt Antonia had been 'quite adamant' about it when Linnie had it made.

I unwrapped the first neatly wrapped bundle that contained a man's black tailcoat, quite elegant, and neatly flat-ironed. I hung it in the wardrobe that had been added to our room, then reached for the second bundle that emitted the faint sound of starched petticoats.

I slowly unwrapped it, almost afraid of what I would find. I needn't have worried, and almost burst out laughing.

It was quite stylish, except for the lace and bows, including one enormous bow on the bodice, the cloth a glorious shade of deep purple reminiscent of the color of her driving costume.

Bravo, Aunt Antonia!

Fourteen

BRODIE WAS UNUSUALLY quiet as he patiently stood while I tied the cravat that my brother-in-law had included with the tailcoat he had sent for him to wear to the reception at St. James's Palace.

There was none of the usual grumbling as I folded one end over the other, made the knot, then widened the satin fabric at his neck and tucked the tails into his shirt.

Nor had there been grumbling earlier when he had returned from meeting with Sir Avery at the Agency Office at the Tower.

He had informed me that all *remedies*, as he called them, had been put in place. Mr. Conner was to accompany Alex to the reception dressed in servant's clothes, along with several other agents selected by Sir Avery, who would be discreet as they moved about the guests in attendance.

Mr. Dooley had been in attendance at the meeting as well to coordinate with men from the MET who might be needed, which was pure 'conjecture,' as Sir Avery had replied when Brodie informed him what we had discovered.

He had demanded to know the source of the information, which Brodie had refused to provide.

According to what he explained to me when he returned several hours later, he told Sir Avery that it was a reliable source, but for safety purposes he could not reveal the name of the person who had provided that information.

I would like to have been a wall-fly during his response. Sir Avery was the sort of person who insisted on being in control of all aspects of a situation.

Not that Brodie didn't have his moments, yet as I had heard him say numerous times—there were many things in an investigation that were beyond control. That included unknown persons involved in a crime, risks that could not be accounted for, and those who waited at the edge of the crime for the outcome.

There had been much discussion about that. He was most adamant about not wanting me to attend the reception, notwithstanding the fact that Aunt Antonia was to attend, along with my sister and her husband.

"I dinna want ye to be part of this," he had made perfectly clear earlier.

It was not the first time he'd made his feelings plain about my involvement in what might possibly be a dangerous situation.

However...

I had pointed out, quite diplomatically I thought at the time, that while he had no practical knowledge of St. James's Palace and the surrounding grounds, I was familiar with the Throne Room where the reception was to be held. As well as the State apartments, though I did not go into detail about my adventures exploring those rooms.

I was just past my fifteenth birthday at the time. Nor did I mention the young man with me who thought to give me a belated birthday present and chose to take advantage, much to his disappointment, considering the black eye I had given him.

If memory served me right, it was not nearly as glorious as Brodie's, which had now faded to a mere shadow above the cut he'd received.

Still, he did cut quite a dashing figure in formal attire, a combination of the proper gentleman and a man who made no claim to be proper. Particularly with that cut just below his eye.

As for the gown I was to wear, I had promptly removed the bows and lace, which exposed somewhat more above the bodice. Even though I was somewhat taller than Linnie, the volumes of purple satin in the skirt disguised it, as well as my black walking boots. Linnie had included a black satin wrap and long gloves. I had left my hair down.

"Will Sir Avery be attending?" I inquired.

"Aye."

He actually spoke! A single word, but an improvement from the silence after our previous 'discussion.'

"Why are you looking at me like that?" I asked and braced for another argument.

"I was thinking how beautiful ye are."

I was highly suspicious. Brodie rarely made compliments, except...those were in private moments. This was somewhat unusual.

"Flattery will do no good," I informed him.

"Is that right?"

"Most certainly."

"Wot if I was to throw ye over my shoulder, carry ye into that room, and have my way with ye?"

"We would be late to the reception. However, you are forgetting an important part to that."

"Wot might that be?"

"What you are suggesting requires two persons."

"Aye. And ye have never been one to object, from the time I found ye on that Greek Island."

"I have no clear memory of that." Although not quite true. "It must have been the ouzo."

Years before...before so many things. And yet he remembered it very clearly.

"Ye were naked as the day ye were born, and I thought I might have been too late in fetching ye back for her ladyship."

"You were not too late, Mr. Brodie. Although there was the possibility of that on the return to London."

"Ye were filled with righteous anger," he replied. "At myself, her ladyship, and threatened to unman me."

I slipped an arm about his neck and gently angled him closer. I did consider his proposal.

"So much the better that I did not."

Yet, I knew him better than he cared to admit. There was nothing I could say, or do, that would prevent him going to the reception. Just as there was nothing he could say that would prevent me.

He pulled me against him, and I felt the anger and the words that he forced back in his hands and the kiss that followed.

Then, unexpectedly, he set me from him.

He had requested the service of Mr. Tavers for the evening. The coach waited as we arrived on the sidewalk below the office.

"Might I say, Mr. Brodie, that you look like a regular toff," Mr. Cavendish commented and received a glare. He grinned. "And Lady Forsythe is like a purple rose."

"When have you ever seen a purple rose?" I inquired.

"I must admit that I have not. Miss Effie is fond of red roses. But I imagine that is what you would look like."

St. James's Palace was in Westminster, not far from the Strand, separated by the Mall that ran between the Palace and St. James's Park.

The evening congestion of the Strand had thinned, and we soon joined the line of private coaches along the parkway lit by gas lampposts, then turned onto the Mall, that was lit as well as the palace. Each carriage and coach in turn approached the main entrance.

St. James's Palace was built more than four hundred years earlier, with three-story red-brick wings that stretched the length of the Mall. At the main entrance was the five-story tower, with an enormous gilt clock rumored to have been a gift from Henry VIII to Anne Boleyn. That was, of course, before he had her beheaded.

While Aunt Antonia had never known the man, due to those five hundred years between, she had not cared for him.

"It is a good thing we are not related," she had once stated. *"William might have been a philanderer, but he was not in the habit of beheading his wives so that he could marry another."*

She was referring to William I of Normandy, our family ancestor. I was not at all certain of the source of her information, but she had been quite adamant about Henry.

"And you must admit that Sir William was far more appealing than Henry. One does wonder how he ever managed to sire children!"

There had been more, specifically to the conversation, as part of my education about the Sword Room at Sussex Square.

However, she carefully censored it in consideration of my young age at the time.

There was a portrait of our mutual ancestor that she had brought from the old fortress, and I had to admit that he was a great deal more appealing than King Henry, who was quite...portly.

We eventually arrived at the entrance and departed the coach.

"Ye will remain," Brodie informed Mr. Tavers, who nodded, then guided the team to the open Mall where other drivers had gathered with their rigs.

Brodie then took my arm and escorted me to the well-guarded tower entrance, where I presented my invitation to the reception. The attendant nodded, and we then entered the formal entrance to St. James's Palace.

The reception, small by comparison to other Royal events, was to be in the Queen Anne Room. We were directed to the Grand Staircase that led to the State Apartments.

Brodie and I had both been inside the royal residence of HRH the Prince of Wales during a previous investigation. However, St. James's Palace was far larger, and the royal residence of the Queen at one time, before she chose to live at Buckingham Palace.

It was considerably more ostentatious, as befitted a monarch, with red carpet, gold balustrades on the grand double staircase, and dozens of gilt-framed portraits of kings and queens over the past four hundred years.

"Wot, no portrait of yer own ancestor?" Brodie commented.

"That was a few hundred years earlier," I replied. "He was quite busy conquering, here briefly, and then departed for France."

. . .

At the top of the first floor was the Guard Chamber, which then led to the Queen Anne Room as well as other State Apartments.

The Guard Chamber contained countless weapons from over the past four hundred years mounted on the walls, one in a particular starburst design with a war shield at the center. We passed glass cases that contained ancient firearms as we followed the procession of guests.

"I was extremely impressed when I first visited the Guard Chamber several years ago."

That dark gaze narrowed as the line slowed while guests were greeted at the entrance to the Queen Anne Room.

"Ye'll not be pulling one of the swords from the wall will ye now?" Brodie commented.

"I will try to restrain myself," I replied as we reached the entrance and were greeted by a footman.

"Lady Forsythe and Guest," he announced.

The 'guest' beside me escorted me into the large reception for the German legation.

After Brodie had returned from his meeting with Sir Avery, we had spoken at length about the reception that lay ahead. I had also made a drawing of the palace, even though it had been some years since I had last visited.

I had included the main entrance, the staircase that led to the State Apartments, the Guard Chamber, and the Queen Anne Room.

We had also made a plan for when we arrived.

Sir Avery's people were to be positioned throughout, posing as guests along with the other attendees, the German legation, the British Prime Minister, the Home Secretary, and other dignitaries.

The Queen was not expected to attend. HRH Edward Albert would be making the formal introduction of the newly appointed German Ambassador, Paul von Hatzfeldt. His Royal Highness would be arriving in a short while.

As we walked around the room, I pointed out those I knew or had heard of through Aunt Antonia.

I avoided most formal functions as they were often boring, stuffy affairs, particularly now with my work with Brodie. I had discovered quite early on, after that first inquiry case, that many were curious about a woman working on private cases. Particularly when there were dreadful crimes, even murder, involved.

The first incident was a supper party my great aunt gave after my sister was found alive and safe.

"Good heavens, the newspaper said that you actually shot the person. However could you do that?" one of her guests had inquired.

"They were escaping," I had replied, perhaps too bluntly.

My response had halted all conversation at the table, as the woman gaped at me. Burke had written that article. The first of several in our somewhat contentious acquaintance.

"And that gentleman with more hair on his face than on his head is Sir Richard Montfort, a member of Parliament and Secretary of State for Foreign Affairs."

I had made inquiries about him after Adele first mentioned him. However, there was nothing at the time to connect him to any of this. He had an impeccable record.

"An important position," Brodie replied, thoughtful.

There were others we knew from past cases, including the

recently appointed Home Secretary, Sir Herbert Gladstone, who exchanged a cordial greeting with Brodie.

Aunt Antonia was presently in conversation with Lord Salisbury as I caught sight of my brother-in-law James as he escorted my sister toward us.

Linnie glowed in a pale-yellow gown with a high waist that disguised her condition, with her blonde hair swept up on top of her head.

"I knew the purple gown would suit you far better than me," she commented as she reached my side and smiled a greeting at Brodie.

"Has Aunt Antonia arrived yet?" she inquired.

"She is presently in conversation with Lord Salisbury," I replied.

"Good heavens," Linnie exclaimed. "Should we rescue her?"

I glanced across the room. "I believe she has the situation well in hand."

"I've not been here in some time," Linnie continued as James struck up a conversation with Brodie. "The paintings are magnificent. There are two Rembrandts here, with another in the gallery."

The Prince of Wales had arrived with Princess Alexandra of Denmark. They greeted officials and guests in a line, exchanging brief conversations. As the line thinned, Linnie and I were joined by Aunt Antonia to make our way to the line and an official greeting.

"The Queen sends her good wishes," the Prince of Wales told my great aunt.

Her acquaintance with Her Majesty was long-standing as they were close in their ages, and the Montgomery family had a long history in Britain, longer even than the Queen's.

It was said by some that Aunt Antonia was responsible for introducing a man of her acquaintance, a Scot no less, to the Queen after the death of Prince Albert. He became a trusted friend and confidant of Her Majesty until his death.

Aunt Antonia had neither confirmed nor denied it, simply explaining to my sister and me that when one lived long enough, there were bound to be rumors. However, she did seem to take great delight in that one.

"The Queen is a woman. Why shouldn't she have a friend and companion. The royals have been notorious for their mistresses and affairs for hundreds of years," she had commented at the time.

HRH was most cordial, as was the Princess of Wales. Brodie had met the Prince of Wales previously in the course of a difficult case that had involved their son, Prince Albert Victor. The case had been solved.

Afterward, HRH Prince Edward had sent a personal letter to Brodie and me, expressing his deep gratitude. Brodie had been surprised, to say the least, as he considered the situation merely part of solving the case.

Yet there was a familiar greeting now, as Prince Edward leaned forward and shared a comment. His expression was quite serious. Brodie seemed to nod in agreement.

"A memento?" His Highness commented, as he seemed to notice the cut below Brodie's eye.

"A scratch, no more," he replied. "The cause hopefully to be remedied tonight."

"I sincerely appreciate your diligence, sir," the Prince of Wales said in parting.

"He seems to be aware of the situation," I commented.

Brodie nodded. "He was informed by Sir Avery."

As the reception line ended, an announcement was made

that the formal recognition ceremony of the new German Ambassador to Britain would take place shortly, with a presentation by the Prince of Wales to acknowledge the continued relationship of good will between the two countries.

At the same time, I couldn't help but think of the reason we were there.

18 April was the date of some importance that Adele had overheard and written in her journal.

I was certain, as was Brodie, that something quite serious was to take place tonight. But what was it?

What had brought three men together at St. John's Wood? And what did that have to do with what Brodie and I had discovered in Portsmouth?

"Be careful," Brodie cautioned as Aunt Antonia approached and he prepared to make his own observations of those who were part of the evening's event. He paused briefly and acknowledged Aunt Antonia.

They did have a special bond, and admittedly, she was responsible for sending him after me when I had *'escaped'* my travel group with one of our guides who promised to show me the ruins on the island.

"It serves you right, my dear," she had lovingly scolded me after I had become part of Brodie's private inquiry cases.

"You had absolutely dreadful taste in men—a Greek guide for Heaven's sake? I despaired that you would ever find a man who could match that wild spirit. I have no idea where you acquired that."

She knew perfectly well.

As for a man who might match my 'wild' spirit?

I admired that lean figure as Brodie crossed the room in that borrowed tailcoat and cravat and found Alex Sinclair on some matter to discuss.

There were other admirers, I noticed, among the ladies he passed. As well as a narrowed glare from the Foreign Secretary, Sir Richard Montfort.

Sir Richard broke off the conversation he was having with a man, and I recognized him as Sir Andrew Smith-Thomas, Lord of the Admiralty.

Sir Andrew was dressed quite formally in a dark-blue tail-coat, much like an officer's coat, with a red sash and sword in the scabbard that hung from under the coat.

I vaguely remembered that he had served in the Royal Navy, as well as having been appointed Lord of the Admiralty.

The conversation appeared quite serious, a question it seemed by the taut expression on the Foreign Secretary's face. And the equally serious response he received. Then, a parting handshake, which seemed oddly unusual for this sort of occasion.

It was a simple gesture between acquaintances when first meeting someone, not in parting. What did that mean? An agreement of some kind?

"See that it is done." I heard the Foreign Secretary say in parting, as I glimpsed something on the edge of his coat sleeve.

Fifteen

BRODIE

"WOT IS IT?" He had caught the subtle signal from Alex Sinclair that told him the young man needed to speak with him.

"Steiner," Alex repeated. "Mr. Conner sent word he's been seen, according to the description that was provided. Near the carriage park on the green."

"No doubt preparin' to leave." And then disappear?

That meant that whatever was to happen tonight had either already taken place or was about to.

He nodded sharply.

"Mr. Conner is waiting at the main entrance."

"Aye," Brodie replied. "Tell Sir Avery wot you just told me, then find Inspector Dooley. His people are coverin' the Mall."

He then asked. "Are ye armed?"

"Yes, sir. And I've earned my proficiency certificate from the men at the Yard."

Brodie shook his head. Even though he had several years on

the young man, he considered them as equals, and that was what he liked about him. He didna put on airs about his work or the man he worked for.

But had he ever killed someone? He doubted it. Being proficient was one part of it, but the other part...takin' a life, was something that stayed with ye. Some were able to handle that part. Others?

"Look for Mr. Dooley and stay with him," he told Alex. "He's had a great deal of experience in these things, and I trust him."

Alex nodded then left.

Brodie glanced about the large reception room, saw Lady Antonia in conversation with James Warren and Mikaela's sister. But was unable to find Mikaela.

He approached James on his way out of the Queen Anne Room, where the Prince of Wales was in an enthusiastic exchange with a guest, surrounded by men.

Brodie recognized several of the men from the MET, as well as a handful of others with the same demeanor, no doubt some of Sir Avery's people sent as a precaution after what they'd learned about those meetings at St. John's Wood.

When he reached Mikaela's family, he pulled James Warren aside and in a quiet voice told him, "Find her."

"Has something happened? What is it?"

James Warren was an intelligent man, suddenly intense. But he also was a studious man who spent his days behind a desk putting out Mikaela's next novel, rather than facing down a dangerous confrontation.

"Take her and yer family over near the Prince of Wales. Stay there until I come for ye."

"Something has happened," James said then. "It's not as if I don't know what your business is, Mr. Brodie. I've read enough from Mikaela's novels and the newspapers. If something has happened, I insist on helping."

Brodie glanced over at Mikaela's sister who stood a few feet away, watching them.

"You can best help by making certain they are safe. And the safest place at present is near His Royal Highness and his guards. But say nothing. With all these people about, I don't want a panic. That is when people get hurt."

James nodded. "I'll find her." And then as Brodie turned to find Mr. Conner, James told him, "Do be careful. I would not want to have to explain to Mikaela if you come to some harm."

He turned then, walked over where his wife stood and gently but firmly took her by the arm.

"Has something happened?" Brodie heard her ask. "James?"

"You and Lady Montgomery will be more comfortable across the room," he told them both. "There are chairs for the ladies, especially in your condition, my dear. I will find refreshment for you."

Brodie left the Queen Anne Room to find Mr. Conner, and then Steiner.

What had happened at their first encounter would not happen again.

~

MIKAELA

Sir Andrew Smith-Thomas nodded curtly as he turned and left by way of a discreet side door at the far end of the reception room instead of the double, while the Foreign Secretary left by those double doors that led to a gallery and State Apartments.

I searched for Brodie but couldn't find him among the guests or with my sister and Aunt Antonia. I glanced back at that side door and made my decision as I crossed the floor and stepped into a narrow hallway that adjoined the Guard Chamber.

That hallway was apparently used by royal staff, or possibly the monarch to escape when a banquet or reception became boring and tedious.

I thought of Henry VIII, who had the original palace built for such occasions, and was known to simply leave a function for his bed with his latest queen or latest mistress.

There were voices as I approached the side door to the Guard Chamber that had not fully closed. Two men were engaged in a conversation, one with a slight accent. The other man was Sir Thomas.

"You must see that this leaves the country without delay," he told the other man, who nodded and replied with that slight accent.

"I will make certain of it. There are people waiting."

Waiting? For what? I thought as I listened.

I glimpsed their exchange inside the Guard Room, the clean-shaven features of the man with the accent, and the mark on the inside of Sir Thomas's wrist as he handed a leather portfolio to the man he spoke with.

It appeared to be a tattoo of the head of an animal, the ears distinct.

A wolf's head?

It was identical to the one the Foreign Secretary hastened to cover with the edge of the sleeve of his tailcoat, and as Sir Thomas turned, light from the overhead fixture gleamed on the gold buttons with that same image scattered across the front of his uniform.

The shorter man with that accent had tucked the portfolio into the front of his own coat and turned to leave.

What was in that portfolio? What was so important that the Lord of the Admiralty had passed it to the man who now crossed the Guard Chamber and would be gone?

Was this what Adele had learned about? Secret meetings held away from London by men of position and power. Then fled, terrified, and had gone to Burke? What was worth a man's life?

What had the other man said? There were people waiting...? Steiner? Others?

Sir Avery had confiscated my pocket revolver, and there had been no opportunity to replace it.

Aggravating man! Along with his comment when Brodie and I were released, that a weapon was a dangerous thing in the hands of a woman.

I had only the slender knife tucked into my boot that Munro had given me.

But if I left to find either Alex or Sir Avery, both men would be gone, as well as whatever was in that portfolio.

I slipped into that ancient armory, the doorway guarded by a pair of crossed lances decorated with royal banners, and on the wall, a satin bell pull that was undoubtedly used in past centuries to assemble the yeomen of the guard for the drawing rooms when it was the residence of the royal family.

I pulled on it even though I had no way of knowing if it was still connected to that ancient, medieval bell system.

The armory reminded me of the Sword Room at Sussex Square, with panels on the walls filled with racks that contained dozens of flintlock rifles, long rifles, and hunting rifles. As well as flintlock pistols and dozens of swords. Along with a sword stand that contained several sabers, as if the men who had once carried them would return any moment.

Sir Thomas had waited several moments after his accomplice had departed, and now followed him, as I reached for one of the sabers.

I do not know if it was the sound of my movement, the rustle of the skirt of my gown, or the faint sound of the blade —that *faint sigh of death*, my instructor had called it. Sir Thomas suddenly stopped and slowly turned.

He laughed, a cold, hollow sound.

"We have not been formally introduced. Lady Forsythe, if memory serves me. Your reputation precedes you."

"What is in the portfolio?" I demanded.

His smile faded.

"It seems that you have seen too much this evening."

I was not surprised that he chose not to answer the question. Still...I needed to buy time with the hope that bell pull might summon someone.

"And the mark on your wrist? A wolf's head, much like the decorations on your tailcoat?"

"You are quite observant."

"The mark of others in that exclusive club that met at St. John's Wood." Not a question. I was through with them.

Not quite as eager to leave now, he turned to face me.

"What do you know about that?"

"Meetings with 'gentlemen' that included the Foreign Secretary and others, that no one was ever to know about. And Steiner?"

A murderer who had already killed once and had tried again with that attack on Brodie.

They had gone to great lengths to keep their meetings

secret at St. John's Wood. It was obvious that no one was to know about their scheme.

The Foreign Secretary, a man in a position of power and influence in diplomatic matters. The man who stood before me, Sir Smith-Thomas, Lord of the Admiralty.

Were there others? Who else was part of this?

His expression changed, from surprise to curiosity.

"You seem to know a great deal, Lady Forsythe."

"And Burke's murder was part of it. He could be persistent." I knew that as well as anyone. "Eliminated, no doubt, because he had discovered something that was supposed to be secret? That threatened to expose all of you. Yet there was one thing you hadn't counted on. That Adele DeMille would go to him. Therefore, she needed to be eliminated as well."

"Things you should not know, Lady Forsythe," Sir Smith-Thomas replied with growing coldness in his voice. "Since you seem to know so much, tell me—where is Mademoiselle DeMille now?"

Not bloody likely, I thought.

"She is safe," I informed him as he moved closer. "As is the journal she kept."

I saw by his reaction that he had not known of it.

Bravo, Adele! I thought. She had written down everything she overheard or saw of those secret meetings at St. John's Wood, even though it might have cost her life.

She had feared that she had sinned because of what she was subjected to while there. She had not! She had survived, as I told her, a miracle with what we now knew.

And now?

I was well aware that it was dangerous and, absurd as it was, I thought of that saying, *'in for a penny, in for a pound.'* I was far beyond a handful of pennies.

"And then there is B-10, in that graving dock at Gosport," I added. "Something you would know a great deal about. Is that what is in the portfolio? Information about B-10?"

Smith-Thomas scowled as he pulled that ceremonial saber from the scabbard under his coat and came at me.

"Far too clever! You will not leave this room alive!"

He came at me, and slashed with that sword...

Sixteen

BRODIE

THE CARRIAGE PARK at the Mall was lit by dozens of gas lamps spread along the parkway and created shadows over the lines of carriages and coaches from those who had arrived for the reception. He waded through them, searching the direction Conner had told him the man matching Steiner's description was last seen.

Among those he searched were drivers and attendants clustered about, cigarette smoke curling into the night air as they casually chatted, stomped their feet against the cold, and waited. Steiner, his size and bulk easily recognizable, was not among them.

Another shadow suddenly appeared, the man tall and thickly muscled by the spread of his shoulders beneath a heavy jacket. The same that Brodie had encountered days before.

Steiner. There was no mistaking him as he stepped out from among those parked coaches with purposeful strides toward the palace.

At a glance, Brodie was aware the others, including Conner, were some distance away.

What was Steiner doing there? And wot reason was he moving toward the palace now?

Questions with no answers. At least not as yet.

He retrieved the revolver from the pocket inside the coat and moved along the edge of the carriage park. And then as Steiner stepped off the curb, he shouted his name.

The man's reaction was immediate as he spun around and scanned the park.

"Stop!" Brodie ordered as he moved toward him.

He'd spare the man and give him a chance to live, in exchange for information he no doubt had about others who might be involved.

Steiner was of a different mind as he lunged back into the shadows of the carriage park.

Brodie went after him as he dodged between coaches. Horses suddenly startled provided the path he took.

The man was surprisingly quick for someone his size, darting past one coach and a surprised driver who cursed at him, then into the shadows of the next row of parked carriages as Brodie followed.

The blow caught him in the shoulders, sending him to the ground and under the legs of a team of horses. He winced with pain from broken ribs as he rolled out from under the horses, then to his feet.

Steiner hadn't remained, but now ran and climbed onto the seat of a nearby coach. The driver, startled from dozing was shoved from the seat.

"Stop!" Brodie shouted, giving the man every chance as he glanced back over his shoulder, then fought to maneuver the team into the open roadway.

Brodie pulled back the hammer of the revolver as he shouted once more for him to stop. Steiner did not look back.

The shot echoed across the carriage park. Then a second shot.

Steiner slumped, then toppled from the coach as others ran up behind Brodie, including Alex Sinclair and Mr. Conner who calmed the horses, then bent over Steiner.

"You haven't lost yer touch, old man. Dead," he told him as they reached Steiner's body. "I didn't like him anyway."

MIKAELA

The tip of his saber sliced the sleeve of my gown, a near miss. He obviously didn't intend for that to happen again.

I heard the faint popping sound from somewhere beyond the palace walls as I brought that ancient saber up with both hands. It was much heavier than a rapier, shorter, but I adjusted as I drove him back with a startled look.

There were no more questions, no need for them. I needed time, even as I heard another sound, very much like a second gunshot. Shouts, and a woman's scream rang out as I moved just out of reach of that sword as Sir Smith-Thomas came at me again.

He couldn't let me escape, nor was I willing to let him escape as I circled again, then lunged, the blade of the ancient sword slicing the front of his coat with those gold buttons.

The skirts of the gown were heavy and awkward as I moved, then moved again refusing to lower the saber for even a moment as he lunged at me. I brought the sword up and blocked his strike.

He cursed and came at me again. Rather than meet that blow, I side-stepped and found that we were where we had begun. Instead of circling away, I raised the sword and drove him back until he was stopped by a display cabinet that prevented any further retreat. I lunged and pinned him with the tip of my saber pressed against his throat.

"How many lives are worth what you've done?" I shouted at him. "And for what? What were you promised? More gold for buttons?"

I was angry...for Adele. And ironically for Burke, who would no doubt have done almost anything for a story to add to his publishing laurels and provide the story of his career. Instead, he had reached out to me as he lay dying...

What will you do now, Mikaela Forsythe?

It would be so easy to end the wretched life of the man before me, sprawled across that display case, his own saber scattered to the floor as he fell back.

"Mikaela."

The sound of my name. Not a shout or a warning, but low, as I had heard it dozens of times as if we were the only two people in that room.

"Ye dinna want to do this, lass."

Brodie... Oh, but I did. I wanted it for Adele, and I suppose that I wanted it for Burke in some small way, even with his endless criticisms, sly remarks about my novels, and his contempt for women in general.

I did so want to end the life of the miserable, cringing man who stared back at me, believing that I could and would.

Brodie reached around me, his hand wrapping around my hands as I held the tip of that saber against Smith-Thomas's throat. It would be so easy.

"Let it be, lass," he said then. "There are others who will see that the man accounts for what he's done."

I slowly lowered the saber as Alex Sinclair arrived, with Sir Avery as well.

"He has a leather portfolio inside his coat that he was given by the Foreign Secretary, Sir Montfort."

"Oh!" Alex replied as he saw the saber I held. "I say! Lady Forsythe! Are you all right?"

I was, and handed the saber to him, which he very nearly dropped and would have hurt himself. He stared at me.

"You might have been injured."

"Ye dinna know her very well," Brodie replied as he slipped an arm about my waist and escorted me from the Armory.

Seventeen

SIX WEEKS LATER...

MIKAELA

I HAD MADE the final edits to the manuscript. It was presently wrapped and bound in brown paper on the seat beside me in the coach as I rode to the offices of Warren & Co., Publishers, to meet with my brother-in-law.

He was most anxious to get it to his editors in time for the release he had planned for October, in time for the winter reading season.

There had already been articles in the newspaper on the Crime Sheet of the Times, in special editions the publisher insisted on putting out. A sort of advertising campaign for the forthcoming book about the scandal involving the capture and exposure of the spy ring, as he called it, in our inquiry case. Those caught included several notable persons, members of Parliament, and the military, plotting to pass on stolen plans for the submarine B-10.

Stories in the newspapers had sent London government

and society into turmoil as the roles of the conspirators were exposed after their arrests.

Sir Smith-Thomas, Lord of the Admiralty, who had access to those plans was arrested the night of the reception at St. James's Palace. Not one to take the entire blame for having stolen the plans, he had willingly shared the names of the others involved in the scheme.

"A coward," Mr. Conner declared when it was revealed that Smith-Thomas had provided the names.

"They never want to take all the blame. Spread it around. It makes them feel just a wee bit better."

Sir Montfort, the Foreign Secretary, was stripped of his position and expelled as a member of Parliament, where he had been privy to highly secret communications with other countries across Europe, had met with foreign Ambassadors, and had initiated foreign policy for Great Britain.

Their goal in taking the plans for B-10, a highly sophisticated underwater vessel—a submarine, as I had first recognized it—was to 'balance the scales' of power. Between those who were increasingly gaining more power across Europe. With the hope of preventing a disastrous confrontation over shipping lanes, ports of call used for commerce, and a growing uneasiness among countries in the Mediterranean and the Far East.

"A harbinger of things to come," Sir Avery had commented in meetings afterward.

Brodie was presently off, meeting with him again. I had declined, in deference to the editing I had promised James I would do. I had no need to hear it all again, while Brodie had been circumspect.

He was not one to condone the things the Agency did and certainly had not forgotten past misdeeds on the part of Sir

Avery. Yet he was pragmatic about things, irritatingly so at times.

"I prefer to know what may be coming at me, rather than stumble into it later when it has become dangerous."

As I was saying, irritatingly so, as I considered some of the things Sir Avery pursued might be issues of the Agency's own making. But I had held my tongue, for the most part due to the fact there were times when Brodie was very much a Scot—stubborn, determined, and single-minded.

I had no idea the reason I put up with all of it...well, actually I did know the reasons.

He was the only man I fully trusted. He was honest, at times painfully so. He understood me as no one other than perhaps my great aunt ever had. He let me grumble and grouse about, speak my opinion. And had prevented me from running Sir Smith-Thomas through, which could have been a bit of a sticky situation. Although at the time, my life was in danger.

There was that other thing...Aunt Antonia had warned me about, albeit with a sly smile.

In the aftermath of the case, it did seem there were times when justice was served.

Sir Richard Montfort, Foreign Secretary, was presently being held on charges of conspiracy and awaiting trial at The Glasshouse Aldershot, under conditions described as medieval. I felt no pity.

Sir Andrew Smith-Thomas, Lord of the Admiralty, facing the same charges for the theft of the plans for B-10, had been sent to Bodmin Prison, Cornwall, to await trial.

For his part, Sir Robert Clinton, Under Secretary to Britain's Ambassador to Germany, had been stripped of his office and recently tried and convicted for his collaboration. He had been the person who was to deliver those plans to his German counterpart.

The full extent of the conspiracy was exposed in the days that followed, as others were found who had contributed to the scheme in one way or another. Not that all were apprehended, as Brodie had explained.

"There are always the ones who live in the shadows and will sell out their mother for the right amount. But a word dropped here or there and they will eventually be found. Or taken care of by others."

For the right amount.

Theodolphus Burke was buried with a service befitting a newspaper reporter with confetti of shredded newspapers. Four people attended, including Brodie and me. It was a trifle sad.

The tailor's assistant, Jardine, was buried as well in a simple grave in the municipal graveyard on the outskirts of Westminster. There was no known family.

As for Adele DeMille, she had been well protected by Mr. Brown, and I was grateful.

She had provided a statement as well as the journal to Sir Avery regarding everything she knew from the time she first went to live at St. John's Wood.

The journal was returned to her when the Agency had all the information it needed. I then promised her that I would write a book based on the journal.

I liked Adele very much, and we had spoken about what was to happen to her now. London held far too many dreadful memories for her. I had suggested a brand-new start.

With that, I had contacted my good friend Templeton, who was presently in a stage production in New York City. We spoke at great length, and she was more than happy for Adele to visit her.

She would introduce her to people she knew, with the possibility of a role in a play. Adele was thrilled at the prospect, with telegrams sent back and forth.

She had left St. John's Wood with little more than the clothes on her back. My sister provided her clothes that she claimed she could no longer wear, 'due to her present condition.'

I had paid for Adele's passage to New York with the sale of that gold button and a little extra pin money. As Sir Smith-Thomas's uniform coat was no longer needed in prison, I persuaded Alex Sinclair to see that it was confiscated, minus the other gold buttons.

Sir Laughton, my family attorney, knew someone who would buy them. The extra money would be deposited into the bank and then funds wired to Adele in New York.

She had left from Southampton the week before and would reach New York in five or six days. She had promised to send a cable when she arrived.

My brother-in-law was thrilled with the project. But our agreement was that the author credit would go posthumously to Theodolphus A. Burke. I suppose it was my way of helping him accomplish what he had aspired to become, a published author, in spite of his often callous and critical remarks about my Emma Fortescue novels.

I arrived in time for my appointment with James at his publishing office. That night at St. James's Palace had enlightened him as to the inquiry cases Brodie and I took on. He had since spoken openly that I should consider a series of murder mystery novels.

"There's a growing audience for those, among the female

readership, of all things." He had been surprised. However, I was not.

More and more, the ladies of my generation were coming into their own. After all, if a woman could be Queen of England...

Next would be the vote for women. I had read that they were making enormous strides toward that in the United States. Britain was next.

"You wrote the book," James reminded me as I handed him the manuscript. "Are you very certain that you don't want credit for it?"

"Quite certain," I replied. "It's the book he would have written, even if our writing styles were very different. And I think it will most definitely help sales with his name on it."

"He was quite well known for his reporting for The Times. And the publisher has agreed to submit a foreword for the book."

"It should be very successful for you."

He had then asked me again about writing a series of mystery novels.

"Sir Arthur Conan Doyle has done exceedingly well. I do believe that it is time for a woman mystery writer. And you certainly have the ability as well as the connections with your work with Mr. Brodie."

I told him I would give it some thought. The idea was most intriguing.

I had Mr. Tavers stop by the bake shop on my return to the Strand, and purchased fresh scones and biscuits.

As I'd left earlier, I got the distinct impression that Rupert was a bit put off that there was nothing for him left from the Public House.

When I finally returned, the post had been delivered, and there was a letter from Lily sent from Edinburgh.

"Perhaps the young miss will be returning soon," Mr. Cavendish commented.

Or not, as Brodie had reminded me more than once. She was no longer a child but an educated, extremely capable young woman. And from that first note when she left, I knew the reason she'd gone was important to her.

Still...

Brodie had returned from his meeting with Sir Avery at the Agency. For the most part, he had recovered from his encounter with Burke's murderer, Herr Steiner.

The cut below his left eye had healed, although it had left a pale scar which I thought made him look rather dashing. When I had teased him about it, he had looked at me with that dark gaze narrowed and a frown. Broken ribs seemed to have healed as well.

Papers on the desk lay before him as he leaned an elbow on the chair's arm, chin propped on his hand, deep in thought.

I set my umbrella in the stand, then crossed the office and laid my bag atop my desk.

"I delivered the manuscript to James. He was quite excited to receive it."

Brodie's response was a mumbled reply.

"He made the suggestion again that I consider writing mystery novels." No response this time as I removed my jacket and hung it on the back of my desk chair.

"How was your meeting with Sir Avery? Is everything all well and good with the end of our case for those stolen documents?"

He finally looked over at me.

"The meeting was not about the case." He sat back, chin

resting on his hand, that dark gaze meeting mine, and that little voice inside whispered there was something more, in that look and in the way he seemed to choose his words.

I called it his 'inspector' demeanor, how he must have appeared when reading a case or interrogating a suspect. Each word carefully considered and measured, as now.

"Sir Avery shared that the Agency has been moving into other areas that it oversees. Our recent case became part of that with certain things that affected, not only the Crown, but had the potential to create difficulties elsewhere."

We had spoken of it afterwards. It was true that several of our cases had included foreign aspects amid growing tensions in Europe and other places.

"He has made a proposal for a new operation within the Agency."

I was immediately suspicious.

"What sort of proposal...?"

Next for Brodie and Mikaela...
DEADLY SACRIFICE

Just a few notes that found their way into Brodie and Mikaela's latest murder mystery.

The end of the 19th century once again saw some amazing inventions as well as growing threats around the world.

Alex Sinclair's code machine was very real, based on the ability to send messages in a series of dots and dashes across telegraph lines several years earlier.

At the time of *Deadly Sin*, that ability had been integrated with underwater cable across the English Channel, along with electricity that allowed for messages to be sent by electric impulses, in a pre-established code.

There was, in the shadows and as a prelude to WWI, a Triple Alliance Agreement between Germany, Austria-Hungary, and Italy to assist each other in espionage, with a growing concern about Britain's colonial interests in far places. I've borrowed that bit of history as a template for what Brodie and Mikaela have faced in this episode of their adventures.

In addition, the development of naval vessels was rapidly advancing. The submarine B-10 was real, deployed by the

Royal Navy in 1906, but in development several years before that.

I've used B-10 as the impetus for the murder of Theodolphus Burke, reporter for The Times of London. As far as the story is concerned, he is given credit for the 'book' published posthumously as a tribute by the woman who was both his nemesis and fascination—Lady Mikaela Forsythe.

The use of the name 'John Doe' had been used by police in Britain for decades for those with no known name or identity. Or by the police as necessary.

I've made reference to Jules Verne. His novel, *Twenty Thousand Leagues Under the Sea*, was considered science fiction at the time and was first published in French in 1870, then translated into English in 1872. I've also mentioned the artist who provided the illustrations for that first publication.

The 'secret' graving dock at Gosport near Portsmouth has played an integral part in the development of Britain's Royal Navy. I found old photographs of the area known as the Solent, with round stone and concrete fortresses with gun batteries positioned strategically to protect Portsmouth. These formed the basis for my description of Gosport with vast warehouses, roads, vans, and wagons of the time.

The tailor's shop in Savile Row is still there. I used it to establish that the wolf's head buttons were created in such a shop.

St. James's Palace became the location for the reception for the German legation, keeping in mind that members of the Royal family had married throughout Europe, including Germany. Queen Victoria's extended family, with the marriages of her sons and daughters, was entwined with European royal families and ambitions, in a world that was rapidly spinning toward change.

And of course, the question—what has brought together the man known only as Torch, the anarchist known as Steiner, and the traitor known as Saber?

Brodie and Mikaela are pulled into the middle of it and drawn into betrayal, conspiracy, and murder with a little help from those they trust, and others not so much.

As the 19th century rapidly draws to a close, times are changing. New inventions pave the way into the future for the Scot and the Lady.

Now, there is that proposal from someone they do not trust so much—Sir Avery of the Agency, that clandestine organization they've worked with in the past out of necessity, even if reluctantly.

Brodie and Mikaela have established a reputation for solving complex crimes that are often not what they seem. Along with the talent and skill for unravelling and exposing far more dangerous schemes.

What is the proposal that Sir Avery has made Brodie? If they accept, where will that now take the private inquiry agent who was formerly with the MET, with his streetwise background for survival? And Lady Mikaela Forsythe, with her connections to the titled class she was born into, her travels, and her novels, along with her penchant for adventure?

And what is happening with Lily Montgomery, the young woman Mikaela brought from Edinburgh and rescued from the dreadful circumstance of her young life?

Why has she now returned to Scotland, a strong-willed young woman, determined to unravel the secrets of the past. Where will that take her and what will she find?

Heartache, betrayal, murder, and...

Angus Brodie and Mikaela Forsythe Murder Mystery

A Deadly Affair

Deadly Secrets

A Deadly Game

Deadly Illusion

A Deadly Vow

Deadly Obsession

A Deadly Deception

A Deadly Betrayal

A Deadly Scandal

Deadly Lies

Deadly Curse

Deadly Ghost

Deadly Attraction

Deadly Murder

Deadly Revenge

Deadly Sin

Merlin Series

Daughter of Fire

Daughter of the Mist

Daughter of the Light

Shadows of Camelot

Dawn of Camelot

Daughter of Camelot

The Young Dragons, Blood Moon

Clan Fraser

Betrayed

Revenge

Outlaws, Scoundrels & Lawmen

Desperado's Caress

Passion's Splendor

Silver Mistress

Memory and Desire

Desire's Flame

Silken Surrender

Angels, Devils, Rebels & Rogues

Ravished

Always My Love

Seductive Caress

Seduced

Deceived

About the Author

"I want to write a book ..." she said.

"Then do it," he said.

And she did, and received two offers for that first book proposal.

A dozen historical romances later, and a prophecy from a gifted psychic and the Legacy Series was created, expanding to seven additional titles.

Along the way, two film options, and numerous book awards.

But wait, there's more a voice whispered, after a trip to Scotland and a visit to the standing stones in the far north, and as old as Stonehenge, sign posts the voice told her, and the Clan Fraser books that have followed that told the beginnings of the clan and the family she was part of ...

And now ... murder and mystery set against the backdrop of Victorian London in the new Angus Brodie and Mikaela Forsythe series, with an assortment of conspirators and murderers in the brave new world after the Industrial Revolution where terrorists threaten and the world spins closer to war.

When she is not exploring the Darkness of the fantasy world, or pursuing ancestors in ancient Scotland, she lives in the mountains near Yosemite National Park with bears and mountain lions, and plots murder and revenge.

And did I mention fierce, beautiful women and dangerous, handsome men?

They're there, waiting ...

Join my newsletter

OLIVERHEBERBOOKS

A small press bound by the belief that every voice matters.

Sign up for our newsletter to learn about new releases and more.
https://oliver-heberbooks.com/subscribe/

Follow us on social media:

facebook.com/oliverheberbooks

instagram.com/oliverheberbooks

amazon.com/oliverheberbooks

youtube.com/@OliverHeberBooksPublisher